The Adoption of Charlie Keenan

A Northern Minnesota Tale of Love, Power, and Prohibition

By

Peggy Ann Vigoren

D1519414

First Edition

The Adoption of Charlie Keenan

Copyright © 2013 by Peggy Ann Vigoren.

This is dedicated to Charlie and Blanche.

Charlie and Blanche Williams in the early fifties having shore lunch on Rainy Lake. Williams Family Photo

International Falls Daily Journal - January 22, 1952.

It was a big night for Alderman Charles Williams. He arrived home at 2 a.m. from a six-hour session of the council. He had barely removed his hat and coat when his wife announced quietly the stork was about to call. He rushed his wife to Falls Memorial Hospital where he put in a 10-house session of pacing the lobby. An 8 pound, 4 ounce, daughter, [Peggy Ann], arrived at noon.

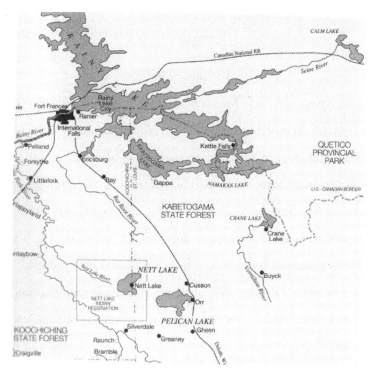

Rainy Lake and Northeastern Minnesota

Introduction

The Adoption of Charlie Keenan is an imaginative re-creation of
events set in northern Minnesota from the years 1907 to
1931. Although a fictional account, it is based as much as
possible on archival sources. The narrative is based upon the
lives of my grandmother, Cora Olsen Keenan, my father,
Charles Keenan Williams, my great-uncle, Arthur Olsen, my
adoptive grandfather, R.S. "Bob" Williams, my adoptive
grandmother, Lil King Williams, my maternal grandparents,
Andrew and Huldah Jespersen, and my mother, Blanche Jespersen Williams.

 The story opens in Duluth, Minnesota, but for the
most part takes place in and around the small city of Ranier,
Minnesota, which lies on the Canadian border where Rainy
Lake runs into Rainy River, and at the Kettle Falls Hotel,
our former family home, which lies fifty miles to the east
where Namakan Lake runs into Rainy Lake.

 I based the storyline on facts taken from birth, marriage, and death certificates, court records, minutes of the Ranier City Council, and censuses. The photograph I saw at

Ranier Picture Day of my grandmother Cora Keenan working at a saw mill in Ranier was a revelation. I relied on old newspaper articles, history books, materials and photos from the International Falls Library and the Koochiching County Museum, materials from the state historical societies of Minnesota and Wisconsin, and the National Park Service to research the history of the time.

Judge Charles LeDuc unsealed my father's adoption papers for a day to allow my sister June and me to review them. The documents form the basis for a great deal of the story of Cora Keenan and how she and my father came to settle in Ranier.

The main storyline came from an outline my father wrote shortly before his death about his early life in Ranier, which was found in his papers. I have attempted to include all of the information from the outline. Other parts of the book are taken from stories my father and mother told my brothers, my sister, and me through the years, and from our parents' oral histories taken by the National Park Service in the 1970s.

The other characters portrayed in this book are based on real people who lived in Ranier and Koochiching County at the time. Most of the references were taken from newspaper accounts and other historical sources, and all the characters living in Ranier were listed on the Ranier censuses from 1910, 1920, or 1930. I used poetic license when I wrote the dialogue and when I entered the mind of a character, but I tried to stay true to the facts of the story and to my research.

I hope you will enjoy looking back at what I found to be a particularly interesting period in the history of the beautiful little city of Ranier, Minnesota, which is strung along the banks of Rainy Lake and Rainy River, and my father's home town.

Thank you.

Peggy Ann Vigoren

Table of Contents

Duluth, Minnesota 1904   Courtesy of Duluth Postcard Collection

Prologue

At the turn of the twentieth century in the thriving city of Duluth, Minnesota, vast fortunes were made in the mining and timber industries. Mansions were built by the industry magnates at a record pace on the east end of Duluth along the banks of Lake Superior. By the year 1907 there were more millionaires per capita in Duluth than in any other city in the United States.

Not only had Duluth become a major hub for the railroad, the city boasted a large harbor, and along with its sister city Superior, Wisconsin was a major port for Great Lakes shipping.

Grand hotels lined Superior Street, the main thoroughfare through downtown Duluth, and lucrative deals were made in the dining rooms and meeting rooms of those hotels by the wealthy timber and mining barons. The vast virgin white pine forests and natural resources of northern Minnesota were being harvested on a grand scale. The Arrowhead Region of northeastern Minnesota was the last area subject to the massive cut-over of virgin timber that had taken place in northern Michigan and Wisconsin in the preceding decades. The largest pine, the white pine often soared to over two hundred and fifty feet, could range from three to five feet in diameter, and could be dated up to five hundred years of age.

Battles would be waged between the industrialists and some of the first conservationists over the damming of the boundary waters and the chain of lakes running along the border of Minnesota and Canada, in order to provide power to the paper mills and saw mills being built in northern Minnesota and southern Ontario.

Immigrants from all over the British Isles and Europe flocked to Duluth to find work in the iron ore mines and in the forests of northern Minnesota. Those that had arrived earlier didn't always welcome them.

The families that had settled in the Duluth-Superior area decades before frowned upon the excessive drinking of alcohol. They were not pleased with the increasing number of saloons cropping up with the coming of the mining and timber booms, and they pitied the wives and children of those who left their paychecks in the saloons.

The rate of alcoholism was astounding throughout the United States at the time and northern Minnesota was not an exception. The population was gradually splintering into the "wets" and the "drys" as the fight for prohibition made its way through the counties and states until it reached the national level.

Many people from different factions believed that alcohol was to blame for most of the country's ills. Those that made their living from the saloons fought the coming of prohibition, and many continued in the business afterwards, becoming criminals in the process. Those well-meaning citizens who worked to bring about the prohibition of alcohol soon found themselves in very turbulent times, bearing witness to the worst crime spree in the history of the country, and the pitting of neighbor against neighbor.

West Duluth 1908   Courtesy of Duluth Postcard Collection

PART ONE: 1907 to 1911

Cora's Dilemma

Twenty-year-old Cora Keenan made her way down First Street in West Duluth through a crowd of people, most who were connected to the railroad in one way or another. Cora attempted to appear inconspicuous as she glanced in the windows of the saloons along the way to see if she could spot her husband, John Keenan. When she didn't see him she was hopeful he had gone to work at the railroad yard that day. He had been picking up shifts loading and unloading boxcars and usually made enough money to pay the monthly rent at Mrs. Jenson's boarding house.

4

West First Street ran parallel to the railroad yard through a neighborhood filled with businesses that catered to the railroad, along with saloons and boarding houses that catered to the working class of the city. This was the poor side of Duluth, but the streets were jammed with people from every walk of life, as the railroad was the jumping off point for the mining and logging booms that were in full swing in the northern part of the state.

When Cora came to the big clapboard house at 1030 West First Street, she climbed the stoop and entered the foyer. She didn't see Mrs. Jenson, the landlady, as she climbed the steep and narrow stairs to the room they had rented on the third floor.

Cora was almost nine months pregnant, and the stairs became harder for her to climb each day. Mrs. Jenson had been good to her, especially as Cora's pregnancy advanced, but she and John had tried her patience on several occasions when they were short or late with the rent, and now it was due again.

Cora opened the door of the rented room and dropped her pocketbook on the bed. This place was a far cry from the Victorian house on the quiet street in Superior where her family lived.[1] There, she had her own bedroom next to her little

---

[1] Wisconsin Census 1895 - Olsen family.

brother Arthur's. She had watched over Arthur since their mother's death when she was five years old and Arthur was an infant. She missed Arthur terribly and felt a tremendous guilt in having left him when she eloped with John.

If John had gone to work today, he should be home soon. Dinner was served by Mrs. Jenson promptly at 6 p.m. On those days when John did not come home on time, Cora's heart sank because she knew he was drinking at one of the many saloons in the neighborhood. Although she knew that Mrs. Jenson meant well, she hated the look of pity on her face on the evenings when John was absent.

Cora waited for John until 6 p.m. and then headed down to the dining room on the first floor. The various boarders were gathered around the table, but John's place was empty. Cora was upset, but she tried not to show it and had her dinner with the others. Each time she held out hope that John might still run in to dinner, late from work, but sober.

After dinner, Cora followed Mrs. Jenson to the kitchen and offered to help with the dishes. "Mrs. Jenson, my husband should be coming home with the rent money soon, but in the meantime could I help you with the dishes?" "Dear, you should be resting in your condition. Be sure to tell me when you feel the baby coming, and we will see that you get to Mrs. Olson's

Maternity Hospital. As far as the rent goes, I will see Mr. Keenan when he comes home." Cora felt a rush of gratitude, "Thank you so much, Mrs. Jenson. I will make it up to you, I promise. I'm sure John will be home soon, and I plan to take in more sewing when I am back on my feet after the baby is born."

Cora fell asleep waiting for Keenan, but he was not there when she woke in the morning. He had often come home late, but he had never failed to come home before morning. When he hadn't returned by that afternoon, Cora went down to the saloon on the corner next to the boarding house to ask if anyone had seen him.

When her eyes adjusted to the light, she saw several men at the bar, but not Keenan. She heard one of the men yell to the bartender, "Me friends will all have a jorem of skee[2] on me!" The men cheered and the bartender laughed, then turned to see Cora standing in the doorway. He stopped short and looked uncomfortable when Cora asked, "Have you seen my husband, Mr. Fulton?" He was obviously not accustomed to seeing a woman in his establishment, but Cora could tell from his reaction that he knew something about her husband's whereabouts. "Mrs. Keenan, I'm so sorry, but I thought you would know that

---

[2] Slang for a shot of whiskey.

7

he left for the Canadian border yesterday. He said he had relatives in Koochiching County and that he was going there to make his fortune."

Cora was shaking from the news as she walked back to the boarding house and climbed the stairs to the room. She looked in the dresser where Keenan kept his few belongings. There in the empty drawer she found a few dollars stuffed in an envelope with a note saying that he was sorry, but that they had made a mistake in getting married without her father's blessing, and that she would be better off going home to her family for the time being. He said that he was sorry he couldn't provide for her and the baby and that he was off to make his fortune in the north. He promised he would send for them.

At first, panic overtook her. She sat down hard on the bed and sat thinking over and over, "What should I do? What should I do?" Cora was afraid of going into labor by herself; the baby was due any day. She missed her stepmother, Bertha. Bertha had always been kind to Cora and her siblings since she had married their father. Cora lay on the bed and thought about her options. After a while, she slept.

Mrs. Jenson checked on Cora later that evening when she did not appear for dinner. Cora wasn't in labor yet, but Mrs. Jenson could tell that something was very wrong. She suspected

8

that Keenan had gone, and when Cora confirmed the fact, she told Cora that she could stay with her until Cora was ready to go to the maternity hospital.

Ida Jenson had never been one to pry into the matters of her tenants. She prided herself on not getting involved in their affairs, but something about Cora touched her heart. Mrs. Jenson had seen her share of couples come and go from her place. She spotted Keenan for the fraud he was the first time she saw him. Tall, with bright blue eyes and dark wavy hair, Keenan was charming and too good looking for his own good. As for Cora, Ida knew the story before it was told; another young woman who had married the wrong man and was paying dearly for it. There was no trace of the happy girl who had burst into her boarding house on her wedding day last September.

Mrs. Jenson brought Cora something to eat and asked her if she could contact her family. Cora replied that her father had been right about Keenan all along and that she couldn't bring herself to face him yet.

On the morning of June 10, 1908, Cora opened her eyes and the events of the previous twenty-four hours came flooding back to her. She was in Mrs. Haldora Olson's Maternity Hospital on the west end of Duluth and she had delivered a baby boy during the night. Mrs. Jenson had helped her to the hospital when she had gone into labor. Where was her baby? The last thing Cora remembered was the nurses taking him away from her and giving her something to make her sleep. The birth had been difficult and the baby weighed over ten pounds; Cora felt lucky to have survived the ordeal. The baby was healthy and beautiful. She decided to name him Charles after her father; she would call him Charlie. Perhaps the gesture would help her father to forgive her.

Cora thought about Mrs. Jenson and her kindness in the days after Keenan left her. When she thought about Keenan the anger she felt for him overwhelmed her. She still had trouble accepting the fact that he had left her in such dire straits. She would find him someday and make him sorry for what he had done.

Mrs. Olson agreed to keep them in the maternity hospital for a few more days, but Cora was in a quandary because she had no money to go back to the boarding house, and she couldn't go to work until she had recovered. It pained her to admit it, but her only option was to ask her father if she could come home. She hoped he would forgive her and that he would let her bring Charlie back home to the family in Superior.

Cora hadn't seen her family since her elopement. Her stepmother had always been good to her, but Bertha had her hands full with five children of her own. Cora's older brother Thomas, a medical student, was still living at home, as was her little brother Arthur, who was now fifteen years old. Her sister Grace and her brother Harry had married and left the house not long before. Cora hoped that she and Charlie could stay in her old room until she could figure out her next move. She would find a job after she got on her feet, and she would save money to set out on her own. She would find a way to go north to the Canadian border and find Keenan. Part of her was relieved Keenan had gone, but now she was left to find a way to care for herself and the baby.

Mrs. Olson came in the room and said, "Mrs. Keenan, the baby is just beautiful! We will be bringing him to you in a few minutes." When Cora held Charlie for the first time, she felt a rush of love that amazed her. She felt as if she had always known this tiny person. For the next few days, Cora and Charlie rested, building up the courage to contact her father and let him know what had happened.

⚜

Cora's father was strict and expected his children to follow the rules of his household. Charles Olsen hadn't always been a hard man, but his children did not often see another side of him. He had enjoyed a comfortable childhood in a loving family in the small town of Honafoss, Norway, where his father, Tor Olsen, was the mayor of the town. Charles's father died suddenly in 1870 when Charles was sixteen years old. Shortly after his death, Charles's mother Cesilie asked Charles to help her to move the family to America. Cesilie Olsen immigrated to the United States with Charles and her younger children, John, Mollie, and Caroline. They arrived in Eau Claire, Wisconsin in the year 1872.

Charles was excited to be in America. He learned the language quickly upon his arrival and applied for citizenship as soon as he was able. As the oldest son, Charles was a serious young man because he understood that the well-being of the family largely depended on him. He was ambitious and by his early twenties had attained an agent's job with the railroad in Eau Claire.

Charles met twenty-two-year-old Cornelia Torgerson in Eau Claire while attending a Sons of Norway meeting. The Torgerson family had emigrated from Norway several years before the Olsen family, and Cornelia had been born in Eau Claire. The serious Charles fell head over heels with the sweet Cornelia, and after asking her father's permission proposed to her in the summer of 1878. They were married in Eau Claire that September. Charles built a house at 219 Madison Street near the river in downtown Eau Claire. The couple looked forward to having a family.

They were not married long when Charles's married sister, Caroline Mason, died, leaving her son, Thomas Mason. Charles and Cornelia took in seven-year-old Thomas shortly thereafter, when his father Hans Mason left for the west.

In their first year of marriage, Cornelia gave birth to their first child Johan, who died when he was ninth months old. Another baby followed the next year, a girl, Cora Margaret, who died a year and a half later. Harry was born in 1883 and Cora Cecelia came four years later in September of 1887, Grace in 1891, and the baby, Arthur, in October of 1893.

Charles was promoted by the railroad and transferred to Superior, Wisconsin, in 1892 when the railroad was extended there. Charles's mother and maiden sister Mollie stayed in the house on Madison Street in Eau Claire, and Charles and Cornelia built a house in the Victorian style in Superior.

Charles and Cornelia were happy raising the family in Superior. Charles Olsen couldn't believe his good fortune in finding such a sweet and lovely wife, but all of that ended when Cornelia died from complications of child birth in November of 1894. Charles was devastated, and left alone to raise his five children, the youngest under a year old. His mother came to Superior to help him, but Charles soon realized that he needed a wife and a mother for the children. He met a childless widow from Superior, Bertha Swanson, and they were married in 1895. Bertha was a kind woman and a good mother to the children. Within the next few years, Charles and Bertha had five children of their own, and by the spring of 1908, the youngest was under two years of age.[3]

---

[3] Olsen family history.

Cora was tall and strong, with gray blue eyes and thick blonde hair. She was sweet, with a fun personality, and there was a time when she could do no wrong in her father's eyes. The usually stern Charles Olsen always had a smile for Cora. Charles Olsen was a proud man, proud of his achievements and appearances meant a great deal to him. He was proud of his adopted son Thomas, who was studying to be a doctor in Superior, but Cora had always been his favorite because she was the picture of her mother.

Cora graduated from Superior High School in the spring of 1905 with excellent marks. She was well liked at school and actively involved in the Daughters of Norway, which pleased her father.

Mr. Olsen had looked forward to Cora making a good match to a man of his choosing. Cora had her share of suitors, but she was headstrong and independent by nature. She was intelligent and valued her education, she read the works of the early feminists, and she believed that women deserved the vote and that people deserved to make a living wage.

Cora also felt that she should be able to pick her own husband, and she considered the idea that she should marry within their circle to be archaic and old-fashioned. After all, they were in America. Cora rejected all of the serious, boring young men that her father considered suitable for her.

In the summer of 1907 the White City Amusement Park in Duluth was all the rage to the young people of the area. Cora and some friends took the trolley to Duluth from Superior on the opening day of the park. There she met twenty-six-year-old John Dickson Keenan, a salesman from Hudson, New Jersey. Keenan approached Cora and flirted outrageously with her. At first she ignored him, but soon she found herself drawn to him, if for no other reason than his nerve and persistence in pursuing her.

Keenan came from a large New Jersey family of English and Irish heritage, and was the polar opposite of the young men Cora had grown up with. He was handsome, charming, and quick to laugh. That evening he saw her home on the trolley and asked if she would meet him again. Against her better judgment, Cora began seeing him without telling her family or her friends. Keenan had recently lost his mother to the influenza. Instead of staying in New Jersey to help his father through a difficult time, he decided to try his luck in the west.

Cora found herself falling for John Keenan, and after knowing him for only a few weeks, she decided to bring him home to meet the family. The look on Charles Olsen's face said it all when he saw Keenan for the first time. He was shocked that Cora was seeing him without his permission. Without taking time to get to know Keenan, he made it clear that he did not approve of him and forbade Cora to see him. Keenan was unacceptable to Mr. Olsen, but Cora defied her father and continued to see Keenan.

On September 4, 1907, Cora packed a suitcase and left the house without being seen. She left a note for her father on the hall table, saying that she was in love with John Keenan and hoped that her father would grow to accept him. They were married that day at the St. Louis County Courthouse in Duluth. Mrs. Josephine Stenberg, the county deputy clerk, and another courthouse employee, Theodore Johnson, were the only witnesses.[4]

The couple rented a room from Mrs. Ida Jenson at her boarding house in west Duluth, and for the first few weeks of the marriage, John was a loving and attentive husband, and in good spirits. His mood quickly changed when he lost his job in sales and had to resort to working physical labor at the railroad yard. Under different circumstances, Cora could have asked her

---

[4] Marriage license John Keenan and Cora Olsen.

father to hire Keenan at the railroad, but that was out of the question.

Keenan was miserable working hard labor and constantly talked about going to the north to make his fortune. He complained about losing his job in sales, blaming his former employer for his troubles. He began to drink in the saloons and didn't try to hide it from Cora. Cora had no experience with alcohol, as it had been forbidden in her father's household except for a birthday or holiday toast. She had never seen John or anyone else intoxicated, and it frightened and revolted her.

Things took a turn for the worse when Cora realized that she was pregnant after only a few weeks of marriage. She was shocked that Keenan was angry with her about the baby, as if it were her fault alone. Cora thought she had loved the charismatic Keenan, but she soon realized he wasn't what he had seemed.

Keenan became more and more distant as the months went by and he spent more and more time in the saloons. Cora tried to put up a brave front, but she was terribly lonely and homesick. Her friends and family were lost to her. When she looked back over the last months, she could see that she had been extremely foolish. She had given up her life, she had caused a scandal that had cost her father his standing in the Norwegian community, and she knew that he would never forgive

18

her for it. She may as well be dead to him; the family was not even allowed to mention her name.

There was no forgiveness in Edwardian society for those who stepped outside of the strict moral codes of the day. Even a rumor of impropriety was enough to ostracize a woman in the strict Norwegian community of Superior. Cora had done much worse; she had married outside of her heritage without her father's blessing. The devastation at the loss of his wife, and now the loss of his eldest and dearest daughter, made Charles Olsen a bitter man.

Five days after delivering her son,[5] Cora sat holding him, waiting outside of the maternity hospital for her father to pick them up. It was a beautiful sunny morning and the lilacs were blooming. Her father would drive the horse and buggy from Superior to Duluth to get them from the hospital. Yesterday, she had sent a telegram telling him that she had a baby and that she wanted to come home. Her father had not answered, but sent word through her brother, Thomas, that he would be coming for her.

---

[5] Charles Keenan birth certificate.

19

Cora wasn't sure how she would tell her father that Keenan had left her and she dreaded the conversation. She was out of money. She needed time to find work and to save enough to set out on her own. She knew she couldn't stay in Superior, where she would be the object of scorn or pity.

Charles Olsen did not speak as he pulled the buggy to a halt, exited, and loaded her suitcase into the back. The nurse handed the baby to Cora when she settled herself next to her father in the buggy. They rode in silence until they were almost to Superior. Cora finally started to explain to her father what had happened, that she was sorry for the trouble she had caused, that she had been naïve and didn't realize the extent of her decision or how badly she had hurt the family. Her father didn't say a word or look at her or the baby.

The tone was sober at the Olsen household and quiet in the big house when they entered. Cora was encouraged that he had let them come back home, but her father had said nothing to her about how long they could stay.

Cora's stepmother Bertha met them in the vestibule, took the baby from Cora, and exclaimed, "What a beautiful big boy!" Bertha led Cora up the stairs to her old room. Relief flooded through her and she was so happy that they were going to take them in. Her things had not been moved; it was just as she left it.

She noticed the cradle next to her bed and the baby clothes on the dresser. Cora hugged Bertha and Bertha responded, "He's not taking this well, Cora. I don't know what will happen, but for now, you can stay." As Bertha busied about the room, tidying the blankets in the crib and parting the curtains, she went on to explain, "We're stretched thin with all of the children. The youngest is just out of diapers; it's been difficult to make ends meet these days. It's put a lot of strain and pressure on your father. I know you didn't mean to hurt him, but he hasn't been the same since you left. He had such high hopes for you."

Cora knew that her father was disappointed in her, and that he had expected her to make a good marriage so he wouldn't have to worry about her; that she may even have helped the family by marrying well. Instead, she had married a man who her father considered to be beneath her, and now the man had deserted her. Her father considered Cora's reputation to be ruined, even if she was married. She realized that she had committed the unforgivable in her father's eyes, and that she had broken his heart.

Cora's brother Arthur was happy to see Cora and he took to Charlie immediately. Cora could not believe how much Arthur had grown in the past nine months. He was sixteen years old and almost as tall as her. Cora could tell that her older brother Thomas was embarrassed by her situation. Thomas worshiped Mr. Olsen, probably because he had taken Thomas in after his mother's death. Cora was sure that Thomas's friends had no idea she was married and had a baby, and he didn't want them to know.

Cora's father had not spoken a word to her by the time she was on her feet again. He left for his job at the railroad office each morning and returned at night without a glance at Cora or Charlie. When she was feeling well again, she began to help Bertha as much as possible with the housework and the children. Cora wanted to earn their keep and was grateful they let her bring her son back home.

Her happiness was short lived because Cora soon learned just how angry her father was. It didn't matter how much she helped with the housework or how hard she tried to make up for her indiscretion. Nothing would have made a difference because her father could not live with the scandal.

One evening not long after Charlie's first birthday, Cora's father came home from work and immediately called her to his study. He informed her that he was taking Charlie to the Superior Children's Home because they could no longer afford to keep him. Mr. Olsen gathered the baby and the small suitcase Bertha had packed with the baby's clothes, walked out the door, and got into the buggy.[6] Cora was beside herself. She followed him to the buggy and begged him to reconsider. "I promise that I will take Charlie and leave as soon as I have enough money saved. What has happened to make you do this? If it is just money, I will get a full time job to pay for us." Her father answered, "I am tired of people coming up to me in the street and making comments about you and your baby. You have shamed this family. When you can afford to keep him on your own, you can take him back." "Who saw him, Father?" Cora asked, "I'm sorry, Father. I won't take the baby out! I will keep him at home and we won't be a bother." "I've made up my mind." He answered, "As far as I am concerned, your name is still Olsen and this incident will be forgotten." He got in the buggy and drove

---

[6] Census for Superior Wisconsin 1910 - Charley Keenan

off without a backward glance. Cora was devastated and angry. Bertha tried to console her, but she would not be comforted.

The next morning, Cora dressed early and walked downtown to the Superior Children's Home. She was determined to see her son. The home was located several blocks from the Olsen house, in a mansion that had been donated by Martin Pattison's widow. Pattison was a mining baron. He built the big house for his wife as a wedding present and the couple raised their six children there. After Pattison's death, his wife Grace wanted to put the house to good use. She donated the big house to be used as a home for orphans in Superior and then left for the east coast.

Cora climbed the large stone steps of the Superior Children's Home and knocked on the massive front door. A maid answered, and as Cora entered she could see that the children were having their breakfast in the dining hall. Mrs. C.G. Moon and Mrs. Ida Anderson, the women who operated the home, greeted Cora and invited her to come in. The women could see that Cora was upset that her father had brought her baby there, and they allowed her to see Charlie. The women met with Cora and they assured her that she could visit Charlie as often as she wished. Cora was grateful and promised that she would be there every day to see her son. She spent the day with Charlie and helped with the other children.

From then on, Cora and her father refused to look at or speak to each other. She no longer sought her father's forgiveness and love. The relationship was ruined for her also and she lived for the day that she would take Charlie and leave Superior.[7] Cora promised herself that she would never again be hurt by a man, and that she would get her son back if it was the last thing she ever did.

The family was divided as to whether their father had done the right thing. Thomas always sided with their father. Arthur sided with Cora and the two of them began to hatch a plot to get the baby back and for Cora to make her escape. Arthur did odd jobs in the neighborhood. Cora had her own sewing machine and was a talented seamstress. She took in sewing from a seamstress in the neighborhood and saved every penny. Cora and Arthur visited Charlie at the children's home almost every day, without their father knowing.

After two long years, Cora was finally ready to make her move. She asked her brother Thomas, who had graduated from

---

[7] Census for Superior, Wisconsin 1910 - Charles Olsen family

25

medical school, if he could lend her some money to add to her savings. Thomas was relieved that she wanted to take the baby and leave. He was only too happy to give Cora all the money that he could.

On June 10th, 1911, Charlie's third birthday, Cora packed their belongings in her trunk and had it sent to the train station in Duluth. Cora asked Bertha to help her to get Charlie out of the children's home. She and Bertha proceeded there to convince the authorities to give Charlie back to Cora. Mrs. Moon and Mrs. Anderson listened to Cora explain her plan to find her husband in Koochiching County on the Canadian border.

Cora was legally married and over twenty-one years old, so the women could see no reason not to return Charlie to Cora. They had been shocked when Mr. Olsen abandoned Charlie there, because they both knew that he had a big family in Superior. The women were very fond of Charlie, they had gotten to know Cora well through her visits with her son, and they considered Cora to be a good mother.

It didn't take long before the papers were drawn, and Cora had Charlie in her arms. Cora hugged Bertha and thanked her for her help. She explained where she was going and promised to write.

Cora felt terrible that she was leaving Arthur, as he had begged to go with her. That morning she had explained to him that she wasn't sure how she would provide for herself and Charlie, let alone the three of them, and that she wanted him to finish school. She left while Arthur was in school, and left him a note saying that she would write to him when she was settled in Koochiching County.

Arthur was upset when he read the note saying that Cora and Charlie were gone. He couldn't understand how their father could let Cora and Charlie go to the frontier alone. By that evening, he was so angry that he confronted him. Mr. Olsen became enraged, and responded by sending Arthur to live with his sister Mollie Olsen, back in Eau Claire, a hundred miles south of Superior.[8]

Cora and Charlie took the trolley to the train station in Duluth. Cora bought a ticket to Ranier, Minnesota, a small town on the Canadian border, which was the closest railroad stop to the city of International Falls where Keenan supposedly had relatives. Keenan's family would surely know his whereabouts, so she would start by finding them.

---

[8] McIntyre Library University of Eau Claire.

As they boarded the train, Charlie laughed and hugged his mother. He had never been on a train before. Cora was terrified of the future, and how they would survive, but she was proud of herself for standing up to her father and for taking her son back.

Ranier, Minnesota circa 1909   Pioneer Hotel   Courtesy of KCHS

PART TWO: 1911 to 1918
The Mysterious Cora Keenan

Cora watched the northern lights from the window as the train chugged north through the night, her son fast asleep on the seat beside her. The conductor had seated them near two families who were on their way home to Ranier. The women, Mrs. Hilke and Mrs. Schmidt, were sisters-in-law, and happy to be returning to their husbands, who were both commercial fishermen on Rainy Lake.[9] Cora envied the ladies who had husbands waiting

---

[9] Oral History of Winston Schmidt by National Park Service.

for them and thought about how different things could have been; then told herself to stop looking back. She had to think positive; it was time to move forward and she was grateful that she and Charlie were together again. Cora had not heard a word from John Keenan since he had abandoned her in Duluth. She doubted that Keenan was still in the area, but she hoped that his family might know of his whereabouts.

The train was due to arrive in the frontier town of Ranier, Minnesota, at 1:00 a.m. Ranier was located at the mouth of the Rainy River, just a stone's throw from Canada. The new city was formed when the new Duluth, Rainy Lake and Winnipeg Railroad reached the Canadian border, at the end of a gold rush at Rainy Lake City, and the beginning of a logging boom in Koochiching County.

The railroad purchased the town site of Ranier from John Holler, who had been one of the first settlers to homestead in the area. In 1907 another early settler, Fred Couture, built the first hotel in Ranier to house the workers who were building the railroad. Mr. Couture sold a successful business in Hibbing, Minnesota, in order to relocate his family to Ranier. He was one of the first people to build a house in Ranier, which was located close to his hotel.

By the year 1911, many other businesses had been built in Ranier to cater to the railroad workers, commercial fishermen and their families, and the lumberjacks, who were all coming to the area in increasing numbers. The boarding houses and hotels were full of men who were either commercial fishermen or had been recruited from Duluth to work in the woods cutting timber. The residents who wished to purchase property in Ranier did so through the Ranier Townsite Company, which was a division of the railroad, and was located in a small building behind the bank building on Spruce Street. Houses were constructed as quickly as possible on both sides of the railroad tracks by the commercial fisherman and business owners. A new two-story school house was completed in 1909 and two city docks were built, one on the end of Spruce Street above the Ranier rapids, and the other on Duluth Street below the rapids. Much of the lumber used in all this new construction was provided by the Shelrud Sash and Door Company, which was located on the point just to the north of the Ranier railroad bridge.

Wooden sidewalks were being constructed throughout the little city and new streets were made to accommodate new construction. Kerosene streetlights lit the way down Spruce Street from the railroad depot south to Duluth Street.

A new railroad bridge spanned the mouth of the Rainy River leading to Fort Frances, Ontario, and had been built to accommodate the railroad that now reached as far as Winnipeg, Manitoba.

Cora watched the barren landscape as the train barreled through the remains of the virgin white pine forest that had been cut over by the timber barons as far north as Virginia, Minnesota. Ranier was located another one hundred miles north, and the forest there was still untouched for the most part, although not for long.

The train stopped several times during the night when problems arose with the tracks. The northern portion of the railroad had been extended from Virginia to Ranier, and had recently been operating for only three years. There were often problems with the gravel base on which it was built, and when the train had to stop, workers would fix the problem with the base and the train would continue on.[10]

The population had exploded in Ranier and in all of Koochiching County with the coming of the railroad, which had opened up the north country of Minnesota to people from all

---

[10] *Taming the Wilderness* by Hiram Drache.

over the world. Before the railroad, few settlers had home-steaded in the area under the Homestead Act. The government had pushed the land as farmland, but those early settlers soon learned that the land was useless for farming, as they found more rocks than dirt. With the beginning of the logging boom, many of the settlers gave up the idea of farming and found work in the logging industry or the new paper mill in International Falls.

Edward Wellington Backus, an industrialist from Min-neapolis, had invested a great deal of money in the area. He built a dam on the Rainy River at the city of International Falls, two miles downriver of Ranier, to harness water power for his new innovative paper mill and sawmill.

Backus had plans to build more paper mills along the border. In order to provide power to his mills, he planned to build sixteen additional dams that would stretch from the Boundary Waters west to the mouth of the Rainy River and fur-ther to Lake of the Woods. There would soon be a movement started to stop the building of the dams and to save the boundary waters southeast of Rainy Lake, led by Ernest Oberholtzer, the young conservationist, who spent his time studying the native culture and canoeing in the wilderness.

Cora wondered how she and Charlie would find a place to stay in Ranier at one o'clock in the morning, but the conductor had assured her that the hotels and boarding houses would be open and people would be at the station to meet the train. Several more hotels had been built since the city was incorporated, but the conductor recommended the Pioneer Hotel operated by the Couture family, and he offered to find Fred Couture for her when the train arrived at Ranier. He considered the Pioneer Hotel to be the safest place for Cora to stay until she could find more permanent lodging. Fred Couture was a good man and a pillar of the community, he was the justice of the peace, but most important, he operated the only hotel in Ranier that did not serve alcohol.

The conductor had known Cora's family since their move to Superior, as he had worked for the railroad for many years. He worried about Cora and her son going to the wild frontier town of Ranier, and he wondered how her father could have let them go there alone. Other than the families of the commercial fisherman living in Ranier at the time, the population consisted mostly of the "sporting element" and the business people who supported it. He had purposely seated Cora near to the only two families on the train so she could make their acquaintance.

The swaying of the train finally lulled Cora to sleep. She awoke with a start when the train stopped and the lanterns were lit. The conductor announced, "Next stop, Ranier!" People of every walk of life began rising and stretching; fishermen and trappers, lumberjacks and millworkers, gamblers and swindlers, gentlemen and ladies, and ladies of the night. Cora gathered Charlie and her train case. When she stepped off the train, Cora entered the chaos of a true frontier town. Here, there were no paved streets and no Victorian houses.

"Hello, Mrs. Keenan. The conductor asked that I see to you. I'm Fred Couture. My wife and I have the Pioneer Hotel down at the Duluth Street landing, and if you need a place to stay, we would like to oblige. We see that you have a little one; we'll load your trunk and bring it to the hotel. Mrs. Couture will be waiting and will help you get settled." Cora, carrying Charlie, followed Fred Couture down the corduroy sidewalk,[11] trying to keep her skirts out of the muddy street.

As Charlie and Cora and the rest of the train passengers passed down Spruce Street, the music from the nickelodeons

---

[11] Wooden sidewalk

came pouring from the saloons. Cora saw two men who appeared to be drunk, tumble from the door of a saloon, swinging at each other and missing. Young, rough looking men were throwing silver dollars at cracks in the sidewalk in some sort of game. Saloon girls hung over the hotel windows, calling to prospective customers. There were saloons, hotels, a barber shop, general stores, a meat market, boarding houses, and houses of ill repute!

Just as they came to the corner of Spruce and Duluth Streets, a young man came out of a saloon and almost ran into Cora. He looked at Cora, bowed and said, "Will you marry me?" He held up a diamond ring that he had just won in a poker game. He laughed, tipped his hat, and walked away.

As they crossed Duluth Street and came to the front of the new American State Bank building, Mr. Couture told Cora not to worry, that the young man hadn't meant any harm and that he was a decent sort, but he warned her there were some rough men in Ranier that she would be best to stay away from. Cora told him that she was a married woman and had no intention of having anything to do with the men of Ranier. "I didn't mean to insult you, Mrs. Keenan, I just want you to know that this is a dangerous place and that you should be careful here."

Mrs. Hilke and Mrs. Schmidt bid them farewell at the corner and continued to their houses.

As Cora, Charlie, and Mr. Couture came nearer to the Pioneer Hotel at the end of Duluth Street, the river and the railroad bridge came into view. Water taxis from International Falls and Ranier docked and dropped passengers at the Ranier city dock. The new railroad bridge rose out of the darkness over the river, outlined by the stars. Charlie looking up at the stars said sleepily, "Look, Mama. It's pretty." "Yes, darling, it is." She said, and held him tight.

Delia Couture had Cora and Charlie settled in a room within minutes of their arrival. As Cora fell asleep to the sounds of the water lapping against the shore, the frogs and crickets, and her son's soft breathing, she thought about the decisions she had made that day and how her life would never be the same. She may have made a big mistake in marrying John Keenan, but she wasn't sorry because it had given her a beautiful son. She would always be angry with herself for letting her father separate her from Charlie, and she vowed she would never leave him again. She was hopeful too; she and Charlie would start a new life here. But first she would try to find Keenan.

The next morning, Cora found Delia Couture in the kitchen and asked her if she knew where to find the Keenan family in International Falls, explaining they were her husband's relations. Delia knew where the Keenan family lived and gave Cora directions to their house; it would be at least a mile walk from the city dock at International Falls. Cora and Charlie had breakfast with the Couture family and Charlie met the Couture boys, Scott and Paul. Charlie made instant friends with Paul, who was his age, and with Scott, who was six years older, a responsible boy who always looked out for his younger brother.

After breakfast, Cora and Charlie were headed out of the hotel toward the Ranier City Dock, when Fred Couture caught up with them and said, "Mrs. Keenan, please be careful walking through the Falls. There has been a strike going on at the paper mill for the last three months and tempers are stretched thin. You should stay away from the mill on Second Street in order to miss the strikers." Cora thanked Mr. Couture and said that she would be careful.

They set off in the water taxi with Mr. Erickson, and headed two miles down the Rainy River to the International Falls City Dock. Cora held on to Charlie tightly, afraid that he would fall overboard. Charlie laughed, hugged her, and tried to squirm out of her arms. "He sure is a handful, Mrs. Keenan." said the kindly Mr. Erickson, chuckling. Cora laughed and said, "He certainly is, Mr. Erickson, but a welcome one."

Charlie Keenan Williams in 1911

Williams Family Photo

International Falls, Minnesota circa 1911   Courtesy of KCHS

International Falls was another boom town that boasted that its "streets were paved with gold." The slogan had been coined when tailings were hauled by barge down Rainy Lake from Rainy Lake City, where there had been a gold rush a decade before.[12] The tailings were used as gravel for the streets. "The Falls," as the locals called the city, was located two miles down the Rainy River from Ranier. Rainy Lake City was located on Rainy Lake, ten miles east of Ranier, and had once been home to over four

---

[12] Tailings are leftover rock from the gold mining process.

hundred people. It was now a ghost town due to the end of the short gold rush.

International Falls had originally been named Koochiching and had been part of Itasca County, but had been renamed when Koochiching County was formed in 1907. By 1911, the paper mill that had been built by E.W. Backus was in full operation, and the logging boom was starting in earnest. Backus's lumber mill was built to accommodate all of the new construction in the area, and also to ship south to provide lumber for the continuing migration of immigrants heading west. Backus had plans to build a series of logging camps in remote areas of Koochiching County, and planned a series of small railroad lines to ship the huge white pine logs to his paper mill and sawmill. He had hired experienced papermakers from other areas to work in his state of the art paper mill, which was the biggest paper mill in the world. With the workers came union organizers, and soon the union took hold.

The main street in the Falls had wooden sidewalks similar to Ranier, the streets were just as muddy, and the atmosphere just as chaotic. There was a lot of building going on to keep up with the people moving to the Falls to work at the new paper mill and the business ventures owned by Backus and others.

Cora couldn't help but notice that every other building appeared to be a hotel or saloon of some sort.

Cora avoided Second Street as Mr. Couture suggested, but as she headed west down Third Street, the main thoroughfare, she noticed a large group of men carrying signs a block off to her right, in front of an impressive brick building, which she surmised was part of the paper mill. She and Charlie walked past and made their way out of the downtown and towards a residential neighborhood on the west side of town where the Keenan family lived. Charlie asked as they walked away, "Who are those people, Momma?" "They are union workers at the paper mill." She answered, "They are trying to build a better life for their families." Cora had been horrified by the recent news of the Triangle Shirtwaist Fire in New York City where so many young women had lost their lives working in horrible conditions. Trade unions were becoming popular in Minnesota and work safety was becoming a major issue.

As Cora walked, she thought about what she would say to the Keenans. When they found the house, Cora knocked and waited until Agnes Keenan came to the door. Mrs. Keenan did not invite Cora into the house until she explained that she was married to John Dickson Keenan, her husband's cousin.

Upon entering, Cora could see that the Keenans were not people of property, but the house was clean and tidy. She explained that she didn't want anything from them other than help in finding her husband. There were children running around the house, and Charlie joined in their play. Mrs. Keenan had been pleasant, so Cora was at least happy that she might expect to be part of a family here. Her hopes in that regard were dashed when Mr. Keenan appeared at the door. He was not friendly and he looked tired.

He told Cora in no uncertain terms that John Keenan was long gone to Canada, that he had left shortly after arriving in the area three years before, and that he had not mentioned any family in Duluth. He said that he had no idea where in Canada he had gone, and that he hadn't heard from him since. Cora had the distinct feeling that he didn't believe her story about being married to John Keenan. Mr. Keenan told her that this town was no place for a woman alone with a small child, and that she would be better off going back to her family.[13]

In a daze, Cora walked towards the downtown with Charlie in tow. By the time she reached the block before the

---

[13] Charles Williams Outline.

river, she was shaking badly. She was in a panic and still digesting the fact that she and her son were without means of support and running out of money fast. She had known in her heart that Keenan was gone, but she had clung to a slim hope that she might find him. Charlie began to complain that he was hungry.

Cora saw a restaurant on the corner near the river, a place called The Dutch Room. Surely the place would have a bowl of soup or stew that she could afford. She realized that she had to watch every penny until she found work. As she entered and her eyes adjusted to the darkened room, she saw that the place was nearly empty, and that it appeared to be a restaurant and saloon. She did notice a handsome young couple having a meal at a table near the door. The young woman looked up as Cora passed by and gave her a smile. The man looked surprised to see a young woman and a child unaccompanied in the saloon, as did the bartender.

As Cora was getting Charlie situated at a table, she asked the bartender if they might order something to eat. The bartender called out to the kitchen, and a handsome, well-dressed young man appeared from a doorway in the back of the room. Cora realized with dismay that it was the young man that had spoken to her last night on the way to the hotel from the railroad station!

Robert Sloan Williams, "Bob" to his friends, was an ambitious, hardworking, and adventurous young man who had made his way to Koochiching County earlier that year. Bob was born in Milwaukee, Wisconsin in 1879, and did a stint in the army during the Spanish American War, where he was wounded. He heard about the logging boom in northern Minnesota while working as a chef at the Palmer House Hotel in Chicago.

Bob was an excellent chef, having been trained at the Palmer after his release from the service in the Spanish-American War. He brought all of his favorite recipes with him and the people in the Falls considered the Dutch Room to have the best food in town. Along with the venison stew that everyone served, Bob fried fresh walleye to serve with his homemade tartar sauce, made the best chicken they had ever tasted in the oven of a huge woodstove, and fried huge steaks in cast iron that draped the platter they were served upon. It was agreed that his corn fritters and homemade bread were unsurpassed. All of this and much more was served family style.

Bob was also a very good gambler, a skill he had picked up in the army; he had made some serious cash in high stakes poker games in Chicago. He had many friends from his time in

Chicago and he had enjoyed living there, but he had been plagued with hay fever for most of his life. When a doctor in Chicago told him that northern Wisconsin or Minnesota would be a healthier place for him to live because the vegetation was mostly pine, Bob set out for the north country.

He traveled through Wisconsin and Minnesota with stops along the way to work at hotels in Ladysmith, Wisconsin, and Park Rapids, Minnesota, before he landed in Koochiching County, where he opened the restaurant in The Dutch Room with his savings. Bob was making a good living from the venture, mostly due to his cooking skills, but also because he was a likable guy. Bob planned to stay in the area and had plans to buy his own hotel as soon as he had the money saved.

Bob heard the bartender call that he had a customer. His heart skipped a beat when he saw the striking blonde and the child he had seen in Ranier the night before sitting at the table. He introduced himself and asked her what she would like to eat. "Some soup or stew perhaps, for my son." Cora said. She appeared to be visibly upset. Bob brought her a glass of water and asked her if she was alright. She looked as though she had been crying, and his first instinct was to try to comfort her, but somehow he knew that she wouldn't welcome it.

Trying not to notice that his friends, Jess and Sadie Rose were sitting nearby and could hear his every word, he asked, "What is your name? Are you new in town?" "My name is Mrs. Cora Keenan," she replied, "and we have just moved to Ranier. I'm looking for employment there." "Please let me know if there is anything I can do to help." Bob told her. Cora nodded her thanks, and she and Charlie ate the venison stew that Bob put on the table. "This is good, Momma!" Charlie said with a big smile. "Yes, Darling, and it's good for you." When they were finished, she brought out her coin purse and asked the price of the meal. Bob tried to refuse the money, but she insisted he take it. Cora thanked him, and she and the child left the restaurant.

Sadie and Jess Rose bid farewell to Bob, and then followed Cora down the wooden sidewalk, as they were also headed to catch the water taxi back to Ranier. Jess Rose was a United States customs officer, and had recently been transferred to Ranier from Baudette, Minnesota. Bob often joked that his friend Jess was such a nice guy that on many occasions when he was stationed in Baudette he carried groceries across the border for the ladies who shopped in Canada. Jess and Sadie had not been married long, and had just finished building their home in Ranier, which was located south of the tracks, close to the Couture's new home. Sadie introduced herself to Cora and Charlie as they walked toward the city dock to Mr. Erickson's water taxi.

Bob watched Cora and Charlie as they made their way down the boardwalk towards the city dock. For the next few days, Bob found himself thinking about Cora, wondering what a woman like her was doing on her own in this wild place. Where was Mr. Keenan? She must be a widow, he thought, because no man in his right mind would leave a woman like her. He knew he wasn't likely to forget her, and decided to visit his friends in Ranier more often in order to learn more about the mysterious Cora Keenan.

Cora and Charlie were back at the hotel by late that afternoon. Cora had enjoyed meeting Jess and Sadie Rose, and they had been encouraging about her finding work in Ranier. Back at the hotel, Fred and Delia Couture were happy to see Cora and Charlie, but they could tell that the trip to the Falls had not been what Cora had hoped. She asked Fred if he could think of anywhere she could apply for work in Ranier or the Falls. She told them that her husband had gone to Canada and that she was going to settle in Ranier. She explained that she was a seamstress, and that she would take in sewing as a sideline, but that she needed to find a steady job in order to support her son.

Fred Couture and his wife knew a lot of people in the area. There was a serious shortage of workers with all of the new businesses springing up, so within a few days, Fred had helped Cora find a job at the Shelrud Sash and Door Factory in Ranier. Fred knew Mr. Shelrud well and recommended Cora to work at the factory.

Fred and Delia also helped Cora to find permanent lodging in the home of the Gibbons family, who lived a few blocks from the hotel on the corner of Main and Spruce Streets. Pete Gibbons owned a team of large work horses and a dray wagon and was busy hauling gravel for the new streets that were being built as the city grew larger. Mrs. Emma Gibbons was two years younger than Cora and had a baby girl named Eilene. Emma was happy to have Cora rooming with them and the two became fast friends.

Cora was happy to learn that the Shelrud Sash and Door Factory hired women, and that women were also working at the paper mill and sawmill owned by Backus due to the labor shortage. Cora had seen the women on their way to work at the factory in their overalls and work boots. Cora was strong physically and she was a quick learner. Within a few weeks she was settled in with the Gibbons and doing well at the sash and door factory. The work was physically exhausting, but satisfying in that Cora was supporting herself and Charlie. The Shelrud family was good to its employees, so Cora liked working there, and the physical labor made her lean and strong. Emma Gibbons watched Charlie while Cora was working and he was happy there.

Charlie met other children in the neighborhood; Fred Couture's boys, Scott and Paul, were his closest friends. But he made friends with the Bohman children, the Hilke children, the Schmidt children, and the Thomas children, all sons and daughters of commercial fishermen who had moved to Ranier from southern Minnesota, where most of them had fished the Mississippi River. Because of changing regulations and because of the railroad coming to the area, the fishermen left the Mississippi to try their luck commercial fishing on Rainy Lake.[14] The lake was teeming with fish and the fishermen were successful. The Ranier

---

[14] Winston Schmidt Oral History.

boat works and docks were filled with commercial fishing boats as it became a major part of the little town's economy.

Some of the business people and hotel owners also had large families, so by the summer of 1911, there were a surprising number of children playing in the streets of Ranier. Martin Emmerson, one of the hotel keepers in the city, had seven daughters between the ages of nineteen and three years old. James Brennan, a hotel and saloon keeper, had three children, and Martin Anderson, a railroad worker, had nine children.

Many of the business owners were single men like John and Harry Erickson, who owned a general store, marina, and a water taxi service, and Mr. Gusby, the elderly shoemaker from Finland. There were five hotels, five saloons, a shoe shop, a hardware store, a general store, a trading post, and a candy store located downtown.[i] Pete and Emma Gibbons lived on the corner of Main and Spruce, close to the factory and sawmill where Cora worked, and across the street from Erickson's Grocery. The Gibbons family grew to love Charlie and Cora, and treated them like family.

Cora also made friends with the next door neighbors, Tom and Helma Beaton, who owned the Ranier European Hotel. Within the next few weeks, Cora met several young women in town at the school socials and while shopping in the neighborhood with Emma Gibbons. Emma introduced Cora to the wives of the some of the business owners, and she liked them all. She particularly liked Mabel Smith, whose husband owned a hotel across the street from the Pioneer Hotel, and who welcomed Cora warmly to Ranier. It wasn't unusual for the hotel and saloon owners to socialize with the other families in Ranier. Frank Malloy from the hardware store and the Erickson brothers were considered to be the most eligible bachelors in town. There were few single young ladies living in Ranier. Lillian Barret, a stenographer for the railroad, lived at the Gibbons's boarding house and rented the room next to Cora. Lillian was a serious young woman, shy and sweet. Cora enjoyed all of her new friends in Ranier.

Cora wrote to Arthur soon after she arrived in Ranier, telling him that she was going to settle in Ranier and that she had failed to find Keenan. When she hadn't heard from Arthur in several weeks, she wrote to her stepmother. Cora was upset when she received Bertha's reply, telling her that Arthur had been sent to live in Eau Claire with their Aunt Mollie.

Cora knew that it was all her fault and she felt guilty she had caused her little brother pain. When she finally heard from Arthur, she was relieved to hear that he was happy in Eau Claire, and that Aunt Mollie was treating him very well. Mollie was a seamstress and had never married. She was always happy when any of her nieces or nephews came to visit her, as Cora had often done in the past. She was grateful to Aunt Mollie for teaching her how to sew.

Mollie was happy to have Arthur living with her since she had no children of her own. Arthur had never known their real mother, and after losing Cora, Aunt Mollie was just what he needed. Arthur was able to play both football and basketball, and he was doing very well in school. Cora was relieved to hear that all was well with Arthur. They remained close to each other through correspondence, and planned for Arthur to come to visit as soon as it was possible.

Everyone in Ranier was abuzz in July of that year about the telephone coming to town. The Ranier City Council had given the Koochiching Telephone Company permission to begin installing the poles and wire. The city was planning to buy a large light plant to provide electricity to the town and a block building was being constructed to house the new light plant. Soon there would be no need for the kerosene street lamps. A fire house and jail were constructed near Brennan's Hotel and a new fire engine had been ordered. So many changes were going on, and modernizations. Several Ranier residents built homes on the north side of the railroad tracks, along the shore of Sand Bay. Others built homes on the south side of town, near the hotel and saloon district.

The city was officially three years old, the same age as Charlie! There was much work to do, and the city was spending a fortune to build the road from Ranier to International Falls. Pete Gibbons and his team were hired to grade the gravel road as it was being built. The city was also installing wooden sidewalks throughout Ranier. The business owners had been required by the city council to construct wooden sidewalks ten feet wide and a foot off the ground. Ranier was a busy, prosperous little town. There was even talk of a trolley line between Ranier and the Falls,[15] although a lot of the residents thought the company was a scam and that it was simply trying to sell land along the route to the Falls.[16]

---

[15] Ranier Minutes from 1911
[16] Charles Williams Oral History.

It didn't take Cora long to fall in love with the little city strung along the shores of Rainy Lake and Rainy River. Although the saloon district of Ranier could be a dangerous and rowdy place, Cora wasn't afraid, and she was happy to have her son with her and a job that she liked.

That first summer, when Cora and Charlie went to the Independence Day picnic with Lillian Barret and Emma Gibbons, she saw Bob Williams there with Jess and Sadie Rose. Cora wasn't sure if Bob saw her or if he even remembered her. She hadn't seen him in Ranier since he still lived in the Falls near his restaurant. She caught his eye as he looked over and he smiled and waved. Cora looked away, but gave him a little wave because he was so pleasant and friendly. She stopped herself from thinking about him, believing she had no right to think of any man. After all, she was still a married woman. Emma noticed the exchange and asked Cora how she knew Bob Williams. Lillian gave her a knowing look. Cora laughed and explained that she had met him at his restaurant in the Falls. Cora put any thoughts of Bob Williams aside and enjoyed the day. Cora and Charlie were particularly enthralled with the Indian powwow, the drums, and the dancing.

Cora and Charlie continued to rent from the Gibbons family and Cora worked at the sash and door factory. She took in sewing on the side, and she and Emma Gibbons enjoyed designing and making their own clothes from pictures in the fashion magazines. Lillian usually joined them each evening after her work day at the railroad depot.

Living with the Gibbons was like living with family. They settled into a good life with good friends. Here, Cora wasn't judged or considered to be a ruined woman. The people of Ranier didn't ask each other too many questions about each other's pasts. There were basket socials and dances at the new school house. There were trips up Rainy Lake on the steamboat *Majestic* to picnic at Rainy Lake City and at other spots on Rainy Lake along the way to Kettle Falls. It was pure joy to Cora to live in such a beautiful part of the world. It was all a great deal of fun and she had never felt so free. Charlie was a happy five-year-old and would start school in the fall.

No one seemed to care what a person did before they came to Ranier, or where they came from. Cora loved the fact that she could work hard here and make her own way for herself and Charlie. Cora saw Bob Williams on occasion at the town socials and dances in Ranier. He usually accompanied his good friend Jess Rose and his wife Sadie, now that Jess was the customs inspector at Ranier. Bob Williams was always pleasant and charming to the ladies of the neighborhood and he soon became a favorite dance partner. All the ladies liked Bob. Cora liked him a great deal herself, but she was careful not to show it.

Ranier continued to be the lively little town Cora had grown to love, but as time went on she began to see that things were changing and that crime was escalating because of the political climate of the time. The fight over prohibition was coming to a head in the county and it was dividing the population.

Charlie was old enough to play outside with the many children in the neighborhood, but Cora worried about him getting hurt or winding up in the middle of one of the frequent brawls that occurred in the saloons. Cora and Charlie were close with the Couture family, and Charlie spent a lot of time with Scott and Paul, the Couture boys. Scott Couture often watched Charlie and Paul when they played outside, as he was six years older. He was responsible and wise beyond his years, very much like his father.

Fred Couture resigned from his position of justice of the peace after a short time and took the job of city clerk. After a few months, Fred decided to run for the office of mayor. William Hitchcock took over the job as justice of the peace and E.J. Weber was appointed as city clerk. John Erickson took the job of constable for a short time, but he resigned after a few months and Andrew Nelson was appointed to the job. It seemed that no one kept the job of constable for very long, as it was a thankless and dangerous task.

Gibbons' house was only two blocks from Couture's Pioneer Hotel, a block from Spruce and Duluth Streets, where most of the saloons and hotels were located. Most of the fighting and raucous behavior occurred at night, but there had been incidents that caused Cora to worry about raising a child there.

As more families moved to Koochiching County to take jobs with the various Backus enterprises and in the logging industry, citizens began to complain about the crime that came with the many saloons located in the business districts of Ranier and the Falls. Not only was alcohol flowing, gambling and houses of ill repute abounded, as there were hundreds of single men working in the woods. On their days off, many of them would head to town to spend their money in the saloons and brothels.

As it had in most areas of the country, the women's temperance movement had made its way to Koochiching County and was gaining momentum. There was a wide call for the prohibition of alcohol, in that liquor was blamed for the many men who spent their paychecks in the saloons and left their families without food. These feelings began to create a division between the saloon owners and the other residents of the area.

Fred Couture won the mayoral election on April 1, 1912, on the platform of reform. He ran for the office because he was worried about the escalating drinking, gambling and solicitation in the saloons and hotels in Ranier. Fred wanted to raise the price of a liquor license, but he garnered little support from the Ranier City Council for the idea. He held the position of mayor until the next year, when he lost re-election to Ed Ek.

Even though Ranier had far fewer saloons than the Falls, by July of 1913 Ranier had gained a reputation for being a rough town. That year, ninety-nine arrests were made in the little town with a population of two hundred; most of the arrests were for disorderly conduct or public intoxication. The newspapers all over the state reported a serious incident in July of that year that shocked the residents and showed them just how dangerous the city of Ranier had become.

Everyone in Ranier knew that Fred Couture wanted to curb liquor sales in the city. He had little success in stemming the gambling and houses of ill repute during his time as Justice of the Peace, Ranier City Clerk, and during his short term as mayor. Because of his concerns, Fred agreed to testify before a grand jury that was called to investigate the lawlessness and debauchery in both Ranier and the Falls.

Delia Couture did not want her husband to testify because she feared retaliation. Fred assured her that he would be fine; he felt it was his duty to try to do something to make Ranier a safer place to raise their children.

Fred told the grand jury that as of late the saloons never seemed to close in Ranier, that there was a lot more illegal gambling going on, and that the ladies of the night blatantly plied their trade in the hotels and on the streets. This did not sit well with the sporting element.

On the afternoon of July 13, 1913, Charlie and several other children were playing near the Couture's hotel with Paul and Scott. It was a few days after Fred had given his testimony. Fred had just finished sweeping the steps of the hotel and gone inside, when a group of men who had been drinking in a saloon up the street approached. They were led by James Kelly, a logger who was particularly buoyed by whiskey. Kelly called out to Mr. Couture who presented himself outside. Kelly asked him if he had testified at the grand jury and Couture stated he had.

Kelly then jumped on Couture and the two wrestled and fought. Couture fell or was pushed off the porch into the muddy street and Kelly jumped on him. Frank Hanley, a witness who had been at the hotel with Couture, tried to pull Kelly off of him. Harold Clark, one of the drunken rowdies, pulled Hanley back and told him to let them fight. It was at this time that Mr. Couture was kicked and beaten by others in the mob. Many of the neighborhood children witnessed the assault, with Charlie and the Couture boys among them. Finally, Ed Ek, the mayor at the time, and W. H. Hitchcock, an older council member who was a carpenter by trade, along with other citizens arrived on the scene and stopped the fight.

The children gathered around Mr. Couture and Scott helped his father to rise. With Scott's help, Mr. Couture made his way to the back of the hotel and entered through the back door. He told his wife that he was alright, but that he had wrenched his back. Kelly, who was still out in front of the hotel, yelled at Couture that he was a dirty rat. Couture yelled back to

61

Kelly that he was drunk and to go home, then retired to bed, saying that he didn't feel well and that his back hurt.

Cora ran down the street to the hotel when she heard what had happened. She found Charlie, gathered him up, and then walked to the back door of the hotel to ask Delia if there was anything she could do to help. She knew that Delia had been worried about Fred giving his testimony because she knew it would anger certain people in town. Delia said that Fred was resting and that he said he would be alright. "I don't know where this will all end," she said.

The next morning Mr. Couture was black and blue, in terrible pain, and could not eat or drink. He was brought to the hospital in the Falls where he died later that day of internal injuries. The funeral was held a few days later in the small Ranier church. Sheriff White interviewed the various people who had witnessed the altercation.

James Kelly, Harold Clark, and nine others who had been in the group were indicted by the grand jury. Mayor Ed Ek was among the nine, but the grand jury found that he had not been involved in the beating. Two indictments for manslaughter were brought against Kelly and Clark; the others were dismissed.

After many postponements, the trial finally took place a year later. That day, Cora and many other Ranier residents attended the trial at the Koochiching County Courthouse. The courtroom, located on the third story of the beautiful new building, was packed to the brim with citizens on both sides of the issue. Delia Couture, Frank Hanley, Scott Couture, and W.H. Hitchcock testified for the prosecution.

The defense stated that the whole thing had been a terrible accident, that the situation had spiraled out of control, and that no one had intended for Mr. Couture to die. Cora and Delia sat outside of the courtroom waiting for the verdict. The jury was back after a couple of hours, and everyone filed back into the courtroom to hear the outcome. To the surprise of many, the jury found Kelly and Clark not guilty, and the two went free.[17]

Fred Couture's death was a life changing experience for all of the families in Ranier, including Cora and Charlie. Scott Couture was twelve years old at the time. After witnessing his father's beating and subsequent death, he then had to endure testifying at the trial. He continued to be the steady boy that he

---

[17] *International Falls Daily Journal*

had always been, but the experience would always remain the most traumatic of his life.

Cora no longer let Charlie play outside unattended with his friends, and all the mothers of Ranier watched their children more closely. Fred's wife Delia never recovered from the loss of her husband and she never remarried. She never forgave the people of Ranier for the manner of his death, and because no one ever paid for the crime. From then on, she refused any kindness or offer of friendship from the people of Ranier.[18]

Cora came home from work one day in the spring of 1915 to find Bob Williams sitting at the Gibbons' kitchen table. Cora was embarrassed to be dressed in her overalls and work boots. Her long hair was braided and wrapped around her head. "Do you mind if Mrs. Keenan and I have a word?" Bob asked. "There is no need for them to leave, Mr. Williams. How can I help you?" Cora asked.

---

[18] Rabbit Island Interview

Bob was obviously uncomfortable, trying to find the right words as not to offend her. "I'm here to offer you employment, Mrs. Keenan. I've just purchased a large parcel of land on the beach road about a half mile outside of town. I'm going to start a gravel business to supply the city and county with gravel for the streets, and I am also opening a restaurant in Brennan's Hotel here in Ranier. I am building a new house on the lake property, and I'll need a housekeeper. You would be perfect for the job, and I'll hire people to help with the heavy chores. You won't have to work such hard physical labor, and you and Charlie can live in the country. I will make sure that Charlie can get to school from there."

Cora thought about the offer for the next several days. She talked to Emma and Pete and asked their opinion. It crossed her mind that Bob Williams might have other reasons for wanting her to go to work for him, but Pete assured Cora that Bob was a gentleman and just needed someone to run his household. Emma agreed. "Cora, he's a good guy. Why don't you give him a chance? You can always come back here if it doesn't work out." Cora thought about what they had said and decided to accept the offer. She and Charlie moved to the new

65

Williams farmhouse in August of 1915.[19] The big white house sat across the road from a large, beautiful beach facing Sand Bay on Rainy Lake. Cora made it perfectly clear to Bob that the relationship was strictly one of business, as she suspected that he had feelings for her. She had earned the respect of her friends in Ranier, and she meant to keep it. She had given the job offer a great deal of thought, and Pete and Emma Gibbons both thought the move would be good for Charlie.

Cora and Charlie both enjoyed living in the big house by the beach. They walked or rode horses each day to Ranier to get the mail from Mr. Oster at the post office, and supplies from Erickson's Grocery. Charlie was seven years old now and doing very well in school. He was big for his age, a good natured, happy child, and he loved living in the country. Cora could see that he was going to grow up to be a handsome man like his father. She would try her best to raise him to be a good man, a man that wouldn't abandon his family. To her delight, many of Charlie's mannerisms reminded Cora of her little brother Arthur, who she missed terribly. Now there was someone who Charlie could look up to. Arthur's last letter was all about his exploits in football and basketball. He had been named all state

---

[19] Adoption notes.

in both sports in his senior year of high school in Eau Claire.[20] In his last letter, Arthur said that he would try to visit soon.

As Charlie grew older, being naturally curious, he began asking his mother questions about the family in Superior and about the whereabouts of his father. Cora did not say much about John Keenan. She told Charlie that his father had left them right before Charlie was born and that he had gone to Canada. She told him that Keenan had promised to send for them, but that she hadn't heard from him since and was not sure of what had happened to him. Cora told Charlie that his father may have planned to send for them, but something had happened to him to prevent him from doing so. She told herself that it was possible after all, but then she remembered that he hadn't had the courage to tell her face to face that he was leaving her. Cora told Charlie that John Keenan had been born in New Jersey and that his mother had come from an old family there by the name of Dickson and Randolph. She explained that his father had

---

[20] *Eau Claire Leader.*

wanted him to be named Charles Randolph Keenan after the family there.

Cora didn't tell Charlie about the Olsen family disowning them or about the Superior Children's Home; she figured there would be time enough to tell him when he was older and because she couldn't bear to hurt him. He seemed to have forgotten about being at the children's home and Cora said nothing to refresh his memory. She knew that sooner or later she would have to tell him the whole story, but she wanted to wait until he was mature enough to understand.

Cora did talk to Charlie about her brother Arthur, saying that he would come to visit someday. She always waited to open Arthur's letters until Charlie was home from school, and the two made a ritual of reading the letters together. In Charlie's mind Arthur had reached hero status. Arthur had graduated from high school in Eau Claire and was attending the university there. He continued to play football and basketball for the university.

In his most recent letter, Arthur relayed that he had joined the ROTC, which made Cora nervous because there was talk of the United States entering the war in Europe that had started in August of 1914, and also because there was a current conflict brewing on the border between Mexico and the United

States over the bandit, Pancho Villa, and his raids across the border into the State of New Mexico. Arthur also wrote that he was thinking of joining the Wisconsin National Guard. Cora was extremely proud of her little brother and enjoyed telling Charlie stories about him.

Life was good at the lake house. Bob was very generous and paid Cora a good salary for her work, and he treated her with respect. Charlie liked Bob very much, and Cora could see that Charlie was beginning to look to him as a father figure. In many ways Bob treated Cora as he would a spouse; he gave her a generous household allowance, and gave her full authority to make purchases for the house. He said that he had enough to do with his business ventures, and that he trusted her to manage his home. Bob hired a couple to help with the work on the farm. George and Marie Bailey lived in one of the outbuildings that Bob had converted to a small house.

Bob had many fine qualities, but Cora knew he was a drinking man. She agreed with the temperance movement in many ways, as she herself had seen what damage alcohol could do to the family. Bob made Cora nervous when he came home at night after he had been drinking. He had always been a gentleman, but she didn't take any chances. She always went to her room and pretended to be asleep when she heard his new motor car come into the drive. She could tell that Bob liked her, and she liked him as well, but she was careful to remain professional and to keep a distance between them. She did not want to ruin her reputation with the people of Ranier, who had befriended her when she had no one.

Throughout 1915, Bob was busy with his new business interests. After he sold his restaurant in The Dutch Room in the Falls, he followed through with his plan to open a restaurant in James Brennan's Hotel in Ranier. After a few months of Bob's operating his restaurant in the hotel, the Brennans decided to leave for California. In April of 1915, Bob bought the hotel with the profits from the restaurant and his gravel business. The new hotel not only had a restaurant, but a saloon on one side of the ground floor. In the middle, there was a small lobby with a front desk. At Bob's request, Cora began to operate the front desk during the day while Charlie was at the new school house that was located at the edge of the south side of town, along the new road to the Falls.

The gravel business turned out to be a huge bonus when Bob bought the land on the beach road outside of Ranier. He knew there was gravel on the land when he bought it, but the large amount turned out to be a very pleasant surprise. Bob sold a lot of gravel to the towns of Ranier and the Falls as the population grew. He began to sell gravel on the west side of Koochiching County because there was very little gravel there. That part of the county was mostly muskeg, very hard to navigate except by river.

In spite of the hardships, the west part of the county was being logged, but it was much harder to get to the timber. It was a different story on the east side of the county where most of the land was high and dry, and where the magnificent Kabetogama Peninsula, rich in virgin white pine, spanned thirty-five miles up Rainy Lake, all the way to Kettle Falls.

Bob was faced with a predicament when he went into the hotel business. Some of his customers, especially the lumberjacks and gamblers, expected to have certain amenities provided in the way of female companionship that weren't necessarily legal. The women that catered to the men had usually rented rooms in the hotels, but since the incident involving Fred

71

Couture, the authorities were cracking down on the owners who allowed the women to ply their trade on the premises. They began making arrests, and Bob had no desire to be among the offenders, so he made a deal to refer his better customers to a businesswoman who had recently moved to Ranier.

Lil King was an attractive brunette with beautiful green eyes. She was intelligent, a good businesswoman, and she dressed in the latest fashions. She was an independent woman who had emigrated by herself from Sweden several years before. She had worked her way across the country and wound up in Ranier in the spring of 1915, where she bought a two story building with a false front across the street from the American State Bank building on the corner of Spruce and Duluth streets. She opened a candy store there, which operated as a front for a more lucrative business upstairs.

Lil was tough, and she maintained a discreet operation. When Bob approached her to ask if they could make a business arrangement, she found herself attracted to him, and she was puzzled when he showed no interest in her.

One day when Cora and Charlie were in town to get groceries and the mail, Cora brought Charlie to buy a candy at Lil's new store. They almost ran into Bob as he was leaving the establishment. It was at this time that it occurred to Cora that Lil was selling more than candy, and that Bob was most likely one of her customers. After that incident, Cora was more determined than ever to keep her distance from him.

Lil, who had witnessed the exchange, could see that Bob had more than a passing interest in Cora and that she was more than a housekeeper to him. His demeanor changed immediately when he saw her. He introduced the two women. Lil now understood why he had not taken more of an interest in her, and she was content to remain his friend and business associate.

No one knew better than Lil King that love could be a complicated business. Even though she found herself attracted to Bob Williams, she had no interest in getting involved with a man who was in love with another woman. If Cora was embarrassed during the meeting, she didn't show it. She smiled at Lil as she and Charlie ordered their candy and she paid little attention to Bob.

It was clear to Bob that prohibition was coming to Koochiching County. The Women's Temperance Union had become even more active in the county, and more and more women could be seen wearing the white ribbons that symbolized prohibition.

In February of 1915, the governor signed the Minnesota County Option Law into effect, which made it possible for residents to petition the county to allow a vote on whether to prohibit liquor sales and possession.

Another state law known as the "Roadhouse Law" was passed in April of that year, which made it illegal for the counties to grant liquor licenses to roadhouses located outside of city limits. Ten saloons in the county were forced to close upon the passing of that law, and the county authorities were already arresting those who hadn't complied.[21]

Although Bob had not been involved in the liquor business until he purchased Brennan's Hotel, he was a shrewd businessman and knew that there was a great deal of money to be made in bootlegging if liquor were ever made illegal. Bob believed that many people would still want to have a drink, even if it was against the law, and that they would be willing to pay a hefty price for it.

Bob began cultivating relationships on the other side of the border in order to gain access and stockpile Canadian whiskey. He acquired more land adjacent to the farm, and he constructed outbuildings with cellars under them to store liquor and

---

[21] Article on County Option Law from MHS

stills. His friends, Frank Keyes and Pete Gibbons, the respective mayors of the Falls and Ranier, were both opposed to the county option law, but both admitted that the tide was turning in favor of it. Even Jess Rose admitted that the law would cause a rise in crime, because he knew that some men would do anything for a drink. He joked with Bob that he would be much busier at work if Canadian whiskey was banned across the border.

The citizens of Koochiching County voted to go dry under the County Option Law in the spring of 1915. State laws of this nature were being passed all over the country, a natural progression towards prohibition on a national scale.

George Watson, the editor of the local newspaper the *International Press*, made it his mission to convince the residents of Koochiching County to vote to go dry. He wrote scathing articles about the evils of alcohol and accused Mayor Keyes of the Falls and Mayor Gibbons of Ranier of turning a blind eye to the debauchery.[22]

While Mr. Watson was at the state capitol to advocate for and report on the prohibition of alcohol, his newspaper office was burned to the ground. There was much speculation after it was reported that the fire was arson, but no one was ever

---

[22] *International Falls Daily Journal*

charged. The lines were being drawn between the cities and Koochiching County.

Pete Gibbons had been elected mayor of Ranier in April of 1914. Later that year, city elections were also held on the issue of prohibition; both the city of Ranier and the Falls voted to stay "wet", but the vote was close. Stating that it was the "will of the people," the mayors of both cities refused to close the saloons, so the county filed an injunction. Saloon owners from the Falls and Ranier appealed the injunction, and the case went all the way to the Minnesota Supreme Court.

Tensions between the Wets and the Drys increased with the passage of the County Option Law, and worsened as the lawsuit between the cities and the county made its way through the high court. Residents accused the mayors of rigging the election by enticing all of the lumberjacks to come in to town to vote wet.

The fight over the county option law between the cities of International Falls and Ranier and Koochiching County came to an end when the cities lost the appeal. On February 4, 1916, the Minnesota Supreme Court ruled in favor of the county.[23]

---

[23] *Int'l Falls and Ranier vs. Cty of Koochiching* (Minn. 1916).

County law would supersede the city ordinances regarding liquor. By May 4, 1916, liquor was illegal throughout all of Koochiching County. The first liquor raid followed shortly thereafter. Sheriff White and his deputies netted sixteen bootleggers, and the fight was on.

On a warm night in August of 1916, Cora woke from a dream with a start, her heart pounding. When she was fully awake and realized where she was, she was flooded with relief. In the dream, she was walking faster and faster down First Street in West Duluth, searching through the saloons for Keenan. She was pregnant, all alone without a soul in the street. Cora got up and walked to the dresser to get a glass of water from the pitcher she always kept in her room. When she saw that the pitcher was empty, she walked downstairs to the kitchen.

As she was filling the pitcher from the hand pump at the sink, she heard the back door slam and realized that Bob was home. He entered the back door and almost ran into Cora as she was headed up the back stairs to her room. Cora could see that he had been drinking, and moved to help him to a chair in the kitchen. He put his arms around her and tried to kiss her. Cora pushed him away gently and told him to go to bed.

As she turned away, Bob asked in a soft voice, "Why don't you like me, Cora? Haven't I always been good to you? Can't you see that I care about you and Charlie? I love you, Cora, can't you see that?" Cora was flustered, "I care very much for you, Bob, but you know that I'm a married woman, even if I haven't seen my husband in years. I have no idea if he is dead or alive, but I can't ruin my good name here by having a fling with you. I have a child to support. I do appreciate everything you've done for us, but you have to forget about me in that way." Cora then added, "Anyway, from the look of things, you are well taken care of in that regard. If you want us to leave, just say so. I do feel that I've done a good job for you here." Bob grabbed his coat. "Cora, sooner or later you are going to have to go on with your life. For the record, I don't know what you think you saw at Lil's. She is a friend and a business associate and that is all. You've done a fine job here and there is no reason for you to leave. I won't bother you again." He went into his bedroom and shut the door behind him. Bob was gone much of the time for the next few weeks. Cora thought more than once of trying to talk to him and to apologize, but then thought it was best to leave it alone. Nothing good could come of it.

One evening that September, Cora awoke to car doors slamming outside of the house. She could see through the bedroom window that Bob was home, and that he had several people with him. There were women among the group, and it was clear that they were in a festive mood. Bob had kept his distance since the night he had told her he loved her, and had rarely been at the house since. In any event, he rarely brought his business home to the farmhouse. Bob hollered as he entered the back door, "Cora, I have guests! We want food and drinks!" Cora dressed quickly, and as she ran downstairs she saw Charlie at the top of the stairs. "Go back to bed, Charlie. Everything is fine."

Cora made drinks and food for the group as they sat around the dining room table. Several of Bob's business acquaintances were there, along with Mayor Frank Keyes of the Falls, who was one of Bob's closest friend in the area. Bob did not look at Cora as he draped his arm around one of the girls. The girl stared up at Bob as he talked with the men. She was very attractive and looked like one of the girls who worked at the saloons in Ranier. She was short and curvy, with dyed red curly hair and big blue eyes. She spoke with a squeak in her voice, and she was dressed fashionably, if a bit flashy to Cora's taste.

Cora asked if she could get anything else for them as she turned and started up the stairs. Bob caught her eye, and announced that he and the girl, Margaret Sullivan, had been married that day and that this was a wedding party.[24] Cora's heart sank and she was shocked at the news, but she recovered her composure, hid her surprise, and congratulated them. It wasn't until she had climbed the stairs and entered her bedroom that the pounding in her heart began to subside and the magnitude of the news hit her. She wondered how this news would impact her and Charlie. What had she done? Then she wondered how Lil King would take the news.

Shortly after Bob married Margaret Sullivan, he hired a woman to help Cora with the household chores. The woman, Carrie Shehan, was about Cora's age and was down on her luck. Carrie was a large woman, kind, with a big laugh. She was a great help to Cora and Charlie took to her immediately. Cora wasn't sure

---

[24] Marriage license Robert Williams and Margaret Sullivan

where Carrie had come from or what she had done for a living, and she didn't ask. Bob said that Carrie was a good person and that she needed a job. Carrie was good company and made the work on the farm more enjoyable for Cora.

As the weeks passed, it was almost as though Bob had forgotten about his new wife. Margaret sat around the farmhouse and was soon very bored. She tagged along with Bob at first, but quickly grew tired of his many business dealings. She kept such late hours that it was difficult for her to rise before noon, and she spent hours painting her nails and pampering herself, waiting for Bob to come home. She followed Cora and Carrie around while they worked and talked incessantly. Cora and Carrie didn't dislike her, they both actually felt sorry for her. Bob was very busy with his businesses and didn't mean to be cruel, but Margaret soon realized that Bob wasn't in love with her.

By December of 1916, Margaret had enough of married life. After only two months of marriage, she packed her bags and headed for the Falls to catch the train to Minneapolis, where she had come from. As she walked out the door of the farm house, she turned and said to Cora, "You do know that it's you he wants, don't you? I can see that you feel the same. As far as I am concerned, you two deserve each other! I might just pay a visit to the sheriff on my way of out town! " Cora, surprised, said, "I'm sorry that you haven't been happy here, but that it has nothing to do with me! I hope you aren't serious about the sheriff." Carrie witnessed the exchange, and after Margaret had gone, she told Cora that they had better mention the conversation to Bob.

Cora had been having her own worries. Her brother Arthur had answered the call of the president and joined the Wisconsin National Guard in June of 1916. A big strong guy; his friends called him "Big Ole." He was in his third year of studies at the University of Wisconsin at Eau Claire and a member of the ROTC, when Pancho Villa began his raids across the border into New Mexico. Arthur enlisted in Company F Third Wisconsin Infantry and was sent to the conflict on the Mexican border in September of 1916. He was made sergeant during the short conflict and returned home to Eau Claire that December.[25]

Soon after his return, Arthur finally made the three hundred mile railroad trip from Eau Claire to Ranier to visit Cora

---

[25] Article from University of Eau Claire about Arthur Olsen.

and Charlie. Although they had kept in touch, they had not seen each other since Cora left Superior five years before. She and Charlie arrived at the train station early on the day of Arthur's arrival. It was snowing, a few days before Christmas. Cora was nervous as she stood shivering in the cold, and she hardly recognized Arthur when he stepped off the train. He was very tall, and had grown to be a handsome man. Her nervousness left her when she looked in his eyes and saw that he hadn't changed; he was the same wonderful brother she had loved so much and who had helped her rescue Charlie. Arthur's gray blue eyes were filled with tears when he took Cora in his arms. She realized with a start that Charlie resembled him. Arthur bent down, shook Charlie's hand, and said how do you do. Charlie was shy and in awe of Arthur at first, but within minutes he was peppering him with questions about being in the army and about Pancho Villa.

Cora hadn't seen much of Bob since Margaret's departure. She wasn't sure what to expect upon their return to the farm house, but to her pleasant surprise, Bob was very gracious and seemed genuinely interested in meeting Arthur. Bob cooked a special dinner for all of them that evening, and they visited around the dinner table.

Cora and Arthur sat up that night and reminisced about the years in Eau Claire and Superior. He brought news that Aunt

Mollie was as feisty as ever. He told Cora about a girl he had met at the university, and that he was looking forward to seeing her in Eau Claire. Grace, Cora's sister, was happily married to a doctor in Minneapolis. Thomas hadn't changed, he said, he was still a pompous ass. They laughed a lot that evening, but also had somber moments when their father's name entered the conversation. Mr. Olsen hadn't changed, and he hadn't learned to forgive. Cora told Arthur not to worry, that she and Charlie were fine. She told him the story of how she came to be at the farmhouse, and assured him that she and Bob were not involved. Arthur liked Bob because it was obvious to him that he cared for Cora and Charlie. Arthur took Cora's hand, and said, "Would it be the end of the world if you were? I think he is a good man, and it is obvious that cares for you, Cora. You can't hang on to the past. You should get a divorce from that bastard so you can go on with your life." Cora looked sad and didn't answer. She got up, gave her brother a hug, and said it was time to turn in.

They all celebrated Christmas together at the farmhouse, and in the days following went sledding and skating on the frozen pond nearby. Bob surprised them all when he purchased a race horse named Hamline J. The beautiful horse was shipped to Ranier by railroad and arrived a few days after Christmas.

Cora had never seen Charlie so happy, and she did not remember a better Christmas. She was grateful they had reconnected, that Charlie had been able to meet and get to know his uncle, and that Arthur and Bob had liked each other.

Arthur stayed with them until New Year's Day. Saying goodbye to him at the train station was difficult, but he promised to visit often now that he was back from the service and living in Eau Claire. They planned a visit after the school year ended in the spring.

Arthur returned to his studies at the university, but had not been there long when on April 6, 1917, the United States declared war on Germany. The Americans had managed to stay out of the war until the spring of 1917, but things escalated when the Germans continued to sink ships carrying Americans in the Atlantic. The United States entered the war on the side of the French and the British. To the Americans, the evil face of the enemy was the German Kaiser. Arthur was called back to military service. He left the university and reported to Fort Sheridan in Illinois, shortly after the declaration in April. In September, after several months of training at the fort, he was sent to France. Arthur had been chosen to train with the troops there, and would meet up with his regiment in the spring when the

American troops would make ready for the front. Cora and Arthur corresponded as they always had, and she prayed every day for his safety.

Lt. Arthur M. Olsen
23rd Infantry 2nd Division United States Army

Meanwhile, the fight over prohibition was heating up in northern Minnesota. In October of 1917, Mayor Frank Keyes of the Falls and Mayor Pete Gibbons of Ranier were removed from office by the governor at the request of the new Minnesota Department of Public Safety and replaced by men from out of the area, picked by the department. The reason given was for non-enforcement of the law, and the two were given the opportunity to challenge the removal by hearing. In the meantime, Henry Toureloite of St. Paul was chosen to replace Mayor Keyes of the Falls, and George L. Halley of St. Paul was chosen to replace Mayor Gibbons of Ranier.

The Minnesota Department of Public Safety had been formed after war was declared on Germany and had been given broad power. It was able to form its own army, the Minnesota Home Guard, to be used in surveillance of alleged subversive activities regarding the war against the Germans, in opposition to labor unions, in discouraging the use of the German language in Minnesota schools, in registering and monitoring aliens, in the suppression of political activities and civil liberties, and in enforcing prohibition of alcohol.

The authorities had not gotten over the fact that the cities of International Falls and Ranier had fought the coming of prohibition and had refused to follow the county option law. George Watson continued his campaign against deposed mayor Keyes in the editorials of his newspaper, the *International Falls Press*, and expounded on the virtues of the Department of Public Safety, saying that "Practical results have been accomplished in many instances ... the adjustment of difficulties between labor and the employees, solving many of the county's liquor problems, and in promoting liberty loan campaigns, and for arousing patriotism through its loyalty meetings."

Sheriff White was also removed from office, and many people were angry because the sheriff was well liked and had done his best to enforce the new laws. Sheriff John P. Wall, the new sheriff brought in by the state, was a hard man and not well liked. Deputy Vic Linsten from Loman, who had an impeccable reputation, was kept on the force, as were Deputies McIntosh, Van Ettan, Reedy, and Day.

Shortly after the new sheriff was appointed, Bob's restaurant was raided, as was every other soft drink establishment in Ranier and the Falls. The county had hired detectives from Minneapolis to sneak into town and go to the soft drink parlors and speakeasies, or blind pigs, as they were called in the area.

Then later the police would show up to arrest the offenders. When the police arrived, somehow Bob's establishment was always free of alcohol. There was always speculation he had been tipped off or that the officers had succumbed to bribery.

In that first raid, sixteen people were charged and several businesses and bartenders from Ranier were included. Cora was dismayed to hear that Johnny Beaton, Jazzbo to his friends and who worked for Bob at times, was one of the people arrested for serving liquor at his brother's hotel in Ranier. The Beatons owned the Ranier European Hotel located next door to the Gibbons, and Helma Beaton had been one of the first women to welcome Cora to Ranier. Johnny had been helping Mrs. Beaton run the hotel since her husband Tom died of a heart attack the year before. Tom Beaton had been having heart problems for some time, he drank too much, and he was overweight.

Cora wasn't sure how she felt about prohibition. She had been all for it after her experience with Keenan, but she could see that the experiment was leading to a rise in crime and to the arrest and downfall of people she cared about. And she worried about Bob being arrested.

Since the beginning of prohibition in the county, Bob had been playing a game of cat and mouse with Deputies Van

Ettan and Reedy, who were both gun ho to arrest the bootleggers. Bob's bootlegging activities were escalating and he had hired several men from Ranier to work for him. He had a bunk house built on the farm and several of the men lived there.

Bob was subtle, so at first the authorities did not suspect him. He had been shipping whiskey from Canada to serve the blind pigs that had sprung up all over the county, and he began stockpiling when it appeared that Canada was going to outlaw the exportation of whiskey because of the war in Europe.

Bob was doing all of this under the nose of his old friend, Customs Inspector Jess Rose. Bob knew this could prove to be a problem because Jess had given an oath to uphold the laws of commerce and to stop any smuggling over the border. Jess was a man of his word. He was also very smart and it wouldn't be easy to fool him for long. Bob began to think of different ways to smuggle liquor across the border without using the railroad through Ranier. Two of Bob's men, who lived close to Jess in Ranier, watched his comings and goings.

Bob began studying the art of making gin and building stills, and he planned to construct a very large still on the farm. The underground cellar his men dug under the large chicken coop attached to the big barn had doors and ladders at both ends; it would be the perfect place.[26]

After only a few months, Mayor Keyes, Mayor Gibbons, and Sheriff White were reinstated to office by the governor. Supposedly disgusted with the whole matter, Sheriff White declined to be reinstated, but agreed to stay on until a new sheriff could be appointed. Within a few months, Deputy Hugh McIntosh was elevated to the office of sheriff. Hughes Van Ettan continued as deputy sheriff and he was much more avid in his pursuit of the bootleggers than the new sheriff. Deputies Van Ettan, Reedy, and Day took the job of cleaning up the county seriously and made many arrests for bootlegging. Sheriff McIntosh was much easier on the bootleggers, as he enjoyed a drink himself.

Soon there were rumors that McIntosh was accepting bribes from Bob and others. Deputy Linsten from Loman informed the county board that he had witnessed McIntosh accepting bribes. McIntosh had not been sheriff for more than a

---

[26] Charles Williams Oral History.

few months before there was a call to Governor Burnquist to remove him from office.

On January 22, 1918 the *Duluth News Tribune* reported: "A petition was brought to Governor Burnquist by E.G. Dahlberg and twenty other concerned citizens of Koochiching County to demand the removal of Sheriff Hugh McIntosh on the basis of both malfeasance and nonfeasance in office."[27] Sheriff McIntosh created another problem for himself when he had called for the state guard to come to International Falls to settle a union strike. The strike ended soon thereafter, and all agreed that there had been no need to call in the guard. He made no friends when it became known that the debacle had cost the county the large sum of $400.[28]

Sheriff McIntosh disappeared the same day the inquiry was made public. According to the newspaper account, McIntosh told his wife that he was going to Ray, Minnesota. He walked out of his home that night in January, and later was seen in Fort Frances, across the Rainy River from International Falls; he was in the company of a conductor on the Duluth, Winnipeg & Pacific railroad, who took the midnight train out of Fort Frances for Duluth. The two were seen in the lobby of the St.

---

[27] *International Falls Daily Journal*
[28] *Taming the Wilderness* by Hiram Drache

Frances hotel a short time before the train left. McIntosh disappeared that night, and no one in Fort Frances or International Falls appears to have seen him since.[29]

The successor to Hugh McIntosh was chosen at a meeting of the county board and McIntosh's resignation was tendered through his attorney. Deputy Hughes Van Ettan was chosen to fill the office of sheriff. Van Ettan announced that the personnel at the sheriff's office would remain the same.

A few officers had succumbed to bribery from the bootleggers, but Van Ettan was not one of them. He considered himself to be an upstanding citizen, and he attended church on Sunday with his wife May. Van Ettan would make it his mission in life to clean up the county and bring the bootleggers and other law breakers to justice, and one of his main objectives was to arrest the man who he considered to be the ringleader, Bob Williams. Bob knew that things were about to change and that he had to be even more careful in his bootlegging activities.

After Arthur's visit, Cora tried to mend the rift between her and Bob. He had been hospitable to her brother and she appreciated

---

[29] *Duluth News Tribune*

it very much. She knew her rebuff had hurt Bob and it was the last thing she had intended. She wished that the circumstances were different, but she was still a married woman. Cora had never considered the idea of divorce until Arthur mentioned it during his visit. She told herself to let things be.

Bob seemed relieved Margaret had gone, and almost embarrassed that he had married a women he had known for a matter of days. He started divorce proceedings against Margaret in the winter of 1917. The divorce was final by September of that year.[30] Cora wondered if Bob had sought solace from Lil King, she could hardly blame him if he had.

Cora and Charlie soon returned to their easy life on the farm. At nine years old, Charlie loved living in the country by the beach. He had good friends in Ranier, and they spent their time between play and school. He helped his mother and Carrie with chores on the farm and went to school at the Ranier schoolhouse with the Couture boys and the other Ranier children. Evelyn Ek, the former mayor's daughter, was his first crush and a good friend. For such a small town, there were a surprising number of children, and the new two story schoolhouse was put to good use.

---

[30] Divorce decree Robert Williams and Margaret Sullivan.

The year 1918 turned out to be a big year for Bob financially. He made several purchases that helped him to improve his bootlegging operation and make ready for national prohibition. Bob bought a Curtis Oriole airplane and hired Dutch Rose, a well-known pilot, to fly it; he constructed a runway far back in the woods behind the farm house.

Bob knew that federal prohibition was coming, as state by state, the prohibition amendment was being passed across the country. He would be ready to ship his product over the Canadian border to parts south by airplane.

His most important purchase that year was that of the Kettle Falls Hotel, which was located almost fifty miles from Ranier at the east end of Rainy Lake, where Backus had constructed two dams, one on the American side of the border and one on the Canadian side of the border. In the spring of 1918, Bob bought the Kettle Falls Hotel from an early settler, Ed Rose, for a thousand dollars and four barrels of whiskey. Kettle Falls would be the perfect place to smuggle liquor across the border by boat. Kettle Falls had been a stopping and meeting place for hundreds of years, first for the native tribes, then for the voyageurs and fur traders, and now for the bootleggers, lumberjacks and commercial fishermen. During the logging heyday more than three hundred people lived at Kettle Falls, in cabins and shacks around the hotel, and many of them were ladies of the night.

By finding more inventive ways to smuggle whiskey across the border under the nose of the authorities, Bob found that his business was growing rapidly and he was making a lot of money, in part because he had perfected the art of making gin, and because of his connections in Canada for purchasing whiskey. He placed movable stills in various places on Rainy Lake on the way to Kettle Falls and he hired more men to man the stills.

As a means of transportation to and from Kettle Falls, Bob bought a large boat that he named the *Mayflower* and hired well known Cap Thompson to pilot it. Cap Thompson was a good friend to Bob and no one knew the lake as well as Cap. The boat was one of the fastest boats on the lake, so chances were slim that the authorities would ever catch him. The boat was also used to haul freight and customers to the hotel, so it would be hard for the authorities to determine when the boat was being used for illegal activities. At least half of the time it was used to haul mail, groceries, commercial fisherman, and lumberjacks to Kettle Falls during the day. The night was another story.

In the spring of 1918, Canada ceased the movement of liquor across the border into the United States, but it didn't stop Bob and the other bootleggers on either side of the border. Not only were they still smuggling whiskey under the noses of the federals, they built even more stills around Ranier and Kettle Falls. Bob tried to stay away from smuggling liquor through the railroad at Ranier because Jess Rose was proving to be very good at smelling out Canadian whiskey.

There were several blind pigs operating near the hotel, one was right at the dock, run by Bob's good friend from Ranier, Eli Lessard. Another one was located in an old hut that sat on the hill above the dock and run by Johnny Beaton. There were three or four more blind pigs scattered in the woods and islands near to the hotel, and the girls plied their trade in all of them.

There were even a few families living near the hotel at the time. The Kampmans, who never left the area for many years, had a little house on the hill near the American dam, and operated a blind pig that was frequented mostly by loggers. The Randolphs, the Langfords, and the Knox families all lived near the hotel.

Oliver Knox had settled in the area many years before and was instrumental in building the Kettle Falls Hotel. He and his wife had a steamboat that made trips to Crane Lake from the hotel, hauling passengers and freight across Namakan Lake. The area was surprisingly busy with many people passing through on the way to Ranier and the Falls via Crane, Namakan, and Rainy Lake.

The number of Canadian and American customs officers was increased along the border, but the fact that the border ran fifty miles down the middle of Rainy Lake made it difficult for the authorities to catch the bootleggers in the act.

Not only was the *Mayflower* faster than the government boats, the federal officers were not as familiar with the lake as Cap Thompson was, especially in the dark of night. Time after time the federals were left far behind by the *Mayflower*, and the federals often got lost on the big lake, or hit one of the many rocks that were just under the surface while in pursuit of the bootleggers.

Bob brought Charlie and Cora with him on the first boat trip to Kettle Falls in June of 1918. The fifty mile trip up Rainy Lake took a little over two hours in the *Mayflower*. The lake was beautiful with its many islands, granite cliffs, soaring virgin white pine, and sand beaches along the shoreline. The vast lake was deep blue in color, overhead there was not a cloud in the sky.

As they drove, Bob pointed out the different commercial fishing camps where the Ranier families lived and fished in the summer.

When they arrived at the dock below the new dam Backus had built at Kettle Falls, Charlie was amazed at the sight. There were at least 100 people at the dock, selling and buying fish, and loading them into big wooden boxes filled with ice. The fish boxes were being loaded into big boats for the trip down Rainy Lake to Ranier for processing and shipping at the fish packing plant owned by Bob's friend, Dan McCarthy. The logging boom was also in full swing, and many of the lumberjacks who worked in the woods nearby lived in shacks near the hotel.

Charlie was especially excited to see the Native American families that came to Kettle Falls by canoe to trade fish, wild rice, blueberries, and furs at Chris Monson's trading post, which was located near the portage to Namakan Lake.

When the *Mayflower* was docked, Bob, Cora and Charlie started up the boardwalk to the Kettle Falls Hotel. The boardwalk was a couple of blocks long and was made of logs that cut through a cranberry bog.[31] Charlie could hear the nickelodeon from halfway down the walk. He ran most of the way and made it to the steps long before the others.

The hotel was a rambling white structure with clapboard siding, a red roof, and a wrap-around screened porch covered with vines. The long porch was filled with green wicker furniture. The lobby had a big barrel stove and round wooden tables for playing cards, and a big upright piano for sing-a-longs. There were nineteen rooms upstairs for rent.

The bar was always open, and packed with ladies of the night, lumberjacks, and commercial fishermen. The kitchen had a huge wood stove for cooking, and the dining room sat sixty people. Bob's employees would serve the same good food as Bob served in his restaurants in Ranier and the Falls.

In order to solve what would have certainly been a major problem, the lake people had an ingenious way of providing refrigeration for perishable foods. During the winter, when the lake was frozen solid, they would "put up ice." This entailed cutting huge blocks of ice out of Rainy Lake with big saws, then loading the blocks on sleds pulled by work horses to an ice house

---

[31] Charles Williams Oral History

that held layers of ice and sawdust, which provided insulation to keep the ice from melting during the summer.

The hotel sat on a hill overlooking a cranberry bog that stretched to the lake; the ice-house sat at the bottom of the hill under a big virgin pine tree. Bob planned to operate the hotel during the summer months and close it in the winter, as the rambling building was too hard to heat in the bitter cold. He planned to split his time between his hotels in Ranier and Kettle Falls. Charlie loved Kettle Falls from the moment he arrived, and that first trip up Rainy Lake with his mother and Bob would always remain one of his fondest memories.[32]

Kettle Falls Hotel circa 1918   Courtesy of KCHS

---

[32] Charlie Williams Outline

Throughout the spring and summer of 1918, Cora paid close attention to the news of the war in Europe. Arthur had written to her faithfully from September to March while he was training with the troops in France; she was proud when she received the news that he had made 2nd lieutenant. The rest of his unit arrived in France in March of 1918 and Arthur met up with them to train them for the front. Arthur spent seven weeks as their instructor, then reported to the 2nd Division and was put in charge of a platoon.

Cora read of the German advance in early May, and knew that the dreaded Hun had crossed the Marne River and taken the town of Chateau-Thierry in northwestern France. There had been intense fighting on the Marne River, and it had not gone well for the allies. She received a letter from Arthur at the end of May when Arthur's regiment marched to Meux, France, but Cora hadn't heard from him since.

On June 1st, Arthur, as part of the 23rd Infantry of the American 2nd Division, led his men on a forced march to defend the Paris-Metz road from the latest German advance. The commanders were worried the Germans would make the push to take the road before the Americans could get there. Fortunately, the 23rd Infantry reached the road before the Germans, and the road remained in the hands of the Allies. The line had also held at Chateau-Thierry, and now Chateau-Thierry formed the tip of the German advance toward Paris.[33]

Arthur led his men into action for the first time on June 3rd, when the 23rd Infantry Regiment was ordered to take Hill 204 near Chateau-Thierry. The 9th Infantry Regiment was sent to take village of Vaux. This was part of the American counter-attack launched on June 3rd and 4th, with the assistance of the French Tenth Colonial Division. The Allies succeeded in pushing the Germans across the Marne River to the village of Jaulgonne. Earlier that month, the battle of Belleau Wood had seen the slaughter of American marines when they were ordered to recapture the wood from the Hun without backup artillery.

At huge cost to the Allies, the Germans had finally been forced out of Belleau Wood and back across the Marne. The combined Chateau-Thierry/Belleau Wood action and the capture of Hill 204 and the city of Vaux brought an end to the last major German offensive of the war. Cora heard from Arthur shortly after the battle and was happy and relieved to learn that he had survived. Aunt Mollie wrote that she received a letter

---

[33] *American Battlefields of World War I*, David C. Homsher

from Arthur dated July 9th, after the capture of Vaux. He stated that he was well and that he was happy to be out of the trenches for the time being, but she had heard nothing since.

At the end of July, news of the second battle of the Marne reached Ranier, but Cora and Aunt Mollie had not yet received word from Arthur. On July 18th the Second Division along with Arthur's regiment had pushed forward through the enemy salient at Chateau Thierry and turned the tide of the war, but there had been extensive casualties. For the first time in four years the Allies had a reason to hope for victory against the Hun. The entrée of the Americans into the war had changed everything for the French citizens. They were amazed at the sight of the American soldiers, young, strong, and incredibly healthy, compared to the tired and worn French troops.

The small villages located along the German border, throughout the country of Belgium, and through northeastern France to the village of Chateau-Thierry, had been overrun by the Germans in the beginning of the war in the summer of 1914. At first, it was believed that the war would be over in weeks, but as time went on, and the Germans came closer and closer, the French citizens were terrified that the Germans would cross the Marne River, and the war would reach the streets of Paris. People from every walk of life were forced to evacuate the homes they had lived in all of their lives. The road through the countryside that led to Paris was filled with refugees, pulling every kind of cart imaginable filled with their belongings. Some of the larger country estates were set up as hospitals by the Red Cross.

All railroad cars in Paris were called to haul the troops to the front to meet the Germans, and every man of fighting age was called to serve. The villages were left with clergy, women and children, and a few very elderly men. After a few months of deadly fighting, the French and English finally pushed the Germans back to Chateau-Thierry, but there, the line had held and a No Man's Land developed in between. Trenches were built and both sides of the conflict dug in. The French villages had been sacked and many destroyed during the German retreat across the Marne.[34] Very few citizens had returned to their homes, but now because of the Americans there was reason to hope.

---

[34] *In the Field of Honor* by Frances Huard

Armistice Day: We will remember you on the 11ᵗʰ hour of the 11ᵗʰ day of the 11ᵗʰ month.

On November 11ᵗʰ, 1918, the Great War came to an end. The people of the United States celebrated all across the country, but Cora still had no word from Arthur. That morning as Cora entered the post office in Ranier and asked Mr. Oster for the mail, she was hoping against hope that someone in the family would have some news of Arthur. Cora was frantic by this time and had been checking the mail every day. She was in frequent contact with Aunt Mollie in Eau Claire and her stepmother in Superior, but no one had heard from Arthur since his letter of the 9ᵗʰ of July.[35]

Cora was sick with worry and prayed that he was still alive, maybe wounded or captured and somehow unable to communicate. He had written often, and then, nothing. Cora knew that the 23ʳᵈ Regiment had been deep in the fighting at Chateau Thierry on the day of the American offensive. She had followed Arthur's regiment in the newspaper reports from the front. Day

---

[35] Letter from Arthur of July 9ᵗʰ, 1918, printed in *Eau Claire Leader*

after day, as the war came to an end, there was still no word from Arthur.

It was Bertha's hand-writing that Cora saw on the letter at the Ranier post office. She took it from Mr. Oster and walked back to the farm without opening it. It was cold that day, but she didn't feel it. She entered the big house and put the letter on the hall table. She walked by it several times, before she took it outside to the bench by the clothesline where the sheets were drying. There she sat and thought of Arthur. She prayed that the letter brought good news, but she couldn't shake a feeling of dread.

Bob and Charlie found her there late that afternoon. Bob could tell that something was terribly wrong; he had never seen Cora like this. At first he thought she was ill, but when she looked up at him with such sadness and pain in her eyes, he could see that something terrible had happened. Bob told Charlie that his mother wasn't feeling well and that she needed to rest. Cora was still clutching the letter in her hand as they led her to her room where she lay on the bed. Bob made her a cup of tea, covered her with a warm blanket, sat in the chair next to her bed, and held her hand.

The tea untouched, after a while she began to talk. Arthur had been killed in the second battle of the Marne at Chateau-Thierry on July 18th. He had led the charge of his platoon against the enemy position on that day and was killed by three shots of machine gun fire. He had survived several battles during the month of June and he had acted heroically throughout the fighting. He died trying to save the lives of the young men who had looked up to him. His body would be shipped home and he would be buried in the Norwegian cemetery in Eau Claire.[36] Along with the letter from Bertha was an article from the Eau Claire Leader describing Arthur's fate.

Cora looked at Bob sitting by the side of her bed as if she were seeing him for the first time. She could see the love he had for her, why had she been so cold to him when she knew he cared deeply for her? Arthur had seen the good in him, why hadn't she? Arthur had always seen the good in people and Cora wished she were more like him. She had let Keenan destroy her life. She had driven Bob to the arms of another woman and suddenly she realized how much she regretted that. Bob had always treated her with kindness and respect, and he had been

---

[36] *Eau Claire Leader*.

like a father to Charlie. She would still be working in the door factory if he hadn't offered her a chance at something better.

She told Bob in a quiet voice how she had been disowned by her family when she married Keenan against her father's wishes; that Keenan had left her ten days before Charlie was born with nothing to her name, and that she had been forced to crawl back to her father. She told Bob that her father had been cruel to them and that he had brought Charlie to the Children's Home in Superior and left him there. Arthur had saved her and Charlie. He had helped her to save money and to rescue Charlie. He had supported her and encouraged her not to give up. She told Bob that their mother had died when Arthur was a baby, and that Cora had been like a mother to him. Arthur was like an angel on earth; kind, good, and strong. He was only twenty-four years old, and he hadn't had a chance to fall in love or have a child, and now he never would. He would be lost and forgotten with so many other casualties of the Great War.

When the tears began flowing and she began to sob, Bob took her in his arms. He held Cora for a long time and tried to think of what to say or do. In those moments, he could tell that something had changed in her. She relaxed and she leaned into him. As Bob looked down at Cora, she reached up and touched his cheek. She thanked him for his kindness and told him that she was sorry for how she had treated him, and that she hoped he would forgive her. She told him about what Arthur had said about him, and that Arthur had liked him very much. Bob replied that he admired Arthur, and that there was nothing to forgive Cora for. "I'm so sorry that I pushed you, Cora. I didn't understand and I didn't realize how much you were hurt by your husband and your father." He went on to say that he didn't blame her for losing trust in men.

Cora told him she had always had feelings for him, but she never thought she would ever admit it, even to herself. For years she had convinced herself that she would never have another chance at love because she was married; she was alone and would always be alone because she had chosen her respectability over any chance of happiness. She had let one terrible mistake define her. She could now see that she had been stupid to waste all of those years because of her pride. "I don't care about my reputation anymore." She said, "If you still want me, I am yours. I hope I'm not too late and that you are not in love with Lil." "Cora, I feel the same way," Bob said, "but I want you to be sure about this. I don't want to take advantage of you, and you need to rest right now. We'll talk in the morning. As for Lil, I love her as a friend, but we don't have that kind of relationship. She is a friend, and that is all. Any fool can see that you are the only woman I have ever loved."

If Cora had learned anything from Arthur's death it was that she should live her life fully and try to be happy. She had wasted so much time! The next morning, Cora boldly told Bob that she had not changed her mind. She put her arms around his neck and kissed him. She looked to see Charlie standing in the doorway with a grin on his face.

Cora and Bob talked for hours that day, making plans. Bob asked Cora to marry him, and when she said yes, he said that he would help her start divorce proceedings against Keenan. The divorce would take some time, but when it was final they would be married, Bob would adopt Charlie, and they would be together as a family. Charlie was heartbroken about Arthur's death. He was happy to hear that Bob was going to be his dad, but it would take time for him to deal with the loss. As for Cora, she felt as though she never would.

PART THREE: 1919 to 1927

Roaring Ranier

Charlie was running around the farmhouse telling his mother to hurry; the horse race was about to begin, and they still had to get across the beach and out on to Sand Bay. It was a beautiful sunny day in the beginning of March in the year 1919. The lake was still frozen solid and the mile long race track had been prepared during the past few days. Bob's horse, Hamline J, was the favorite to win. Mayor Keyes also had a horse in the race, as did the Burnett Brothers and several other business owners in the area.[37]

Bob had taken his gambling to another level when he purchased the racehorse, but Cora had long ceased to worry about Bob's gambling. He didn't gamble to excess, and he always seemed to come out a winner. A lot of money was riding on the race, and there was excitement in the air as Cora and Charlie made their way across the ice to where the crowd was gathered near Houska's Point on the northeastern edge of Ranier.

---

[37] Charlie Williams Outline

Within minutes, a gunshot started the race! People were lined up along the track, cheering the horses on. Hamline J. completed the mile in two minutes and twelve seconds to win the race. Charlie and Cora were yelling at the top of their lungs. Bob smiled and waved at Cora and Charlie as he collected his winnings.

Things had been going well for Bob and Cora; they got along well and they were looking forward to the future. As time went on and as she resigned herself to Arthur's death, little by little Cora began to return to her happy self. Every day there were more moments when Arthur was not on her mind. Charlie was a happy ten-year-old; big for his age, handsome, good-natured, with a great sense of humor. He always tried to cheer his mother when he would see the sad, far-away look in her eye.

A few of the women in Ranier treated Cora differently when it became known that she and Bob were engaged, but most of the women were happy for Cora. Her good friends Emma Gibbons and Helma Beaton stood by her. Bob hired Frank Palmer to represent Cora in her divorce from Keenan. Since Keenan's whereabouts were unknown, it would take at least a year for the divorce to be finalized.

Cora had taken Arthur's death very hard, and Bob had seen her through a very difficult time. She hadn't talked to anyone in her family but Aunt Mollie since Arthur's death. Since her father disowned her when she had taken Charlie and left Superior, she supposed that the family had been told not to communicate with her.

Aunt Mollie wrote that later in the year the University of Eau Claire was planning to honor Arthur for his sacrifice. There would be a public ceremony in the Eau Claire Auditorium dedicating a large portrait of Arthur in uniform that would hang in the administration building of the university. Members of Arthur's regiment collected the money to purchase the portrait, and one of Arthur's friend's from his platoon, Clarence Cleasby, planned to give the speech and unveil the portrait. Cora planned to make the trip to see Arthur honored and she vowed she would not let her father keep her away.

LIEUTENANT ARTHUR M. OLSON

The ex-service men of the school decided at a meeting held on November 11, 1920, to have made a life-size picture of Lieutenant Arthur M. Olson, the only man from this school who was killed in the service. the picture to be hung in the assembly hall. In order to raise the necessary money, two representatives were sent to each classroom in the school to ask the assistance of the rest of the students. The response to this call was so generous that more than the necessary amount was raised.

On April 6, 1921, four years after the declaration of war, the unveiling ceremony took place. At this ceremony, the following program was carried out:

America...*By the School*
Address—Loyalty ....*Bailey Ramsdell*
      Eau Claire Post Commander American Legion
Pledge of Allegiance...................*Led by Miss Mabel Segelhurst*
Life and Character of Lieut. Arthur Marcus Olson...*Clarence A. Cleasby*
Unveiling of Picture......................*President H. A. Schofield*
Star Spangled Banner..............................*By the School*

The following is the life history of Lieutenant Olson as given by Clarence A. Cleasby at the unveiling exercises:

In compliance with the request of the committee in charge of this ceremony, it becomes my duty as a comrade-at-arms of the late Lieutenant Arthur Marcus Olson to give you, on this occasion, a brief history of his life. It is altogether fitting and proper that this history should be known to the students of the Eau Claire State Normal, because it was from this school that he entered the service of our country.

Page Forty-two

115

Lieutenant Olson was born in Superior, Wisconsin, on September 18, 1893. He spent his childhood in that city, and came to Eau Claire when he was twelve years of age. He lived with his aunt, Miss Mollie Olson, on East Madison Street, until his entry into the service. In this city, he completed his common-school education at the Eighth Ward School. He then entered the Eau Claire High School. Here he won fame as an athlete, and for four years played football and basketball on high school teams. His nickname, "Big Ole," tells us that he was big; and he was big physically, mentally, and morally. He was also a leader in his school and was admired and respected by all.

In 1916, at the call of the President, he enlisted in Company E, Third Wisconsin Infantry, and went to the Mexican border with that company. He was made a sergeant in this organization. It was at this time that I became a comrade of his, and soon learned to admire the fine qualities which he possessed. Among these qualities was a strong will, a will which made it possible for him to do things, to concentrate all his energies toward one end and to accomplish whatever he put his hand to. Although but slightly older than the rest of us, it was to him we would carry our troubles and disputes. He was the man to whom the rest of us looked. His advice to us was always tempered by a personal interest. Another quality was that of taking care of his health. He always kept himself in condition. These are some of the qualities that made him the leader of men that he was. It was impossible to know him and not admire and like him. During all my army experience, I never met a man who was better fitted to lead and to command.

In December, 1916, he returned from the border with his company. He now went about completing his education and further fitting himself for life. He entered this school; but he had not been here long before war with Germany was declared. He was sent to Fort Sheridan, where after three months of training he was commissioned a second lieutenant. He was soon after sent to France, being among the first men to go. Upon his arrival overseas in September, 1917, he attended several French and English army schools. When his old company arrived overseas, he was assigned to that organization as instructor. He stayed with us for seven weeks, teaching us in the art of war and inspiring us with his presence. As soon as our training was completed, he was ordered to report to the Second Division. He was assigned to Company F of the Twenty-third Infantry. In July, the famous battle of the Marne or the Chateau Thierry "Push," the turning point of the war, took place. Into this action went the Second Division. In this division, Lieutenant Olson had charge of a platoon, and it was on July 18, 1918, while leading his platoon in a charge against the enemy position that he was killed, shot in three places by machine-gun bullets. At the time of his death, he was but twenty-four years of age.

Our school has cause to be proud of such a man. When we have left this school and look back upon the days spent here, let us not forget the man from this school who made the supreme sacrifice for his God and his country. Let his life inspire us with the same loyalty and the same Americanism.

Bob was bootlegging on a larger scale, and Cora was worried more than ever that he would be arrested. He was careful to hire all of his work done, and he only hired people from Ranier. He had always been good to the people of Ranier; there was always a meal at either of Bob's restaurants or a few dollars for any of his friends who were down on their luck. He also paid very well, and therefore he didn't worry that his employees would rat on him to the police.

Bob gave away a lot of money to charity and even made large donations to St. Thomas Catholic Church in the Falls. Bob had been raised as a strict Catholic. His mother, Ella Williams, still lived in Milwaukee and visited Bob on occasion. He always accompanied her to church, and she was proud of him when he purchased a beautiful stain glass window for the church in her name. Mrs. Williams was pleased when the priest patted Bob on the back and said, "Bob is a good boy."

Bob's front for his bootlegging was his gravel business and his hotels in Ranier and Kettle Falls, but by the fall of 1918, he wasn't fooling anyone. Word had gotten around and Sheriff Van Ettan now believed that Bob was responsible for a great deal of the whiskey that came across the border from Canada in

117

the area as well as a large amount of the gin made on the Minnesota side. Bob had frustrated and made an enemy of Van Ettan, who would stop at nothing to catch him.

Bob was as discreet in his dealings as he could be, but people in a small town talk and the people of the area were beginning to realize the scope of Bob's business. *The Daily Press* reported, "One night the new sheriff received a tip that a suspicious cart of hay was in route to Ranier. The sheriff and his officers lay in waiting for the unloading, expecting to nab several barrels of booze. They were doomed to disappointment as the large cart had been opened before its arrival and the wet goods extracted."

The next day, Van Ettan and Reedy paid a visit to Bob at the restaurant in Ranier, and warned him that sooner or later he would slip up and they would catch him. He had made a fool out of both the officers too many times, and they would stop at nothing from then on to catch him. Cora often told Bob he shouldn't antagonize them, but Bob was enjoying himself too much to stop. None of this escaped the notice of Jess Rose.

Bob bought another boat to haul customers and supplies to Kettle Falls in the spring of 1919. He purchased the *Elizabeth B* from E.W. Backus, renamed it the *Mayflower II*, and hired a young boat captain from Ranier to operate it. Bob, Cora, and

Charlie spent most of that summer at Kettle Falls. Bob found a partner from Orr, Minnesota, by the name of Rusty Reeves. Bob's operation expanded, as Rusty helped Bob ship the liquor from Kettle Falls through Namakan Lake to Crane Lake, and then on to the train at Cusson, a wild logging and railroad town located sixty miles south of the Canadian border.

In July of 1919, Billy Noonan wrote in the *Baudette Region*, "Dark thought; Ninety in the shade, and prohibition. There is a lot of unemployment, but it isn't in the bootleg industry."

As Bob's business grew, his customers often visited Bob in order to check merchandize and to get away from it all. Shipping whiskey outside was legal again in Canada after the war ended in Europe.

Bob's pilot was already flying booze to St. Paul, Kansas City and St. Louis for the outrageous price of $300 per case.[38] Dutch Rose flew the plane to Winnipeg, Manitoba, picked up the whiskey, and then flew south to make deliveries. The plane

---

[38] Koochiching Museum Paper on Prohibition

would return to Bob's farm and land on the runway he had constructed in the woods behind the farm, in order to pick up the cases of gin that Bob made there in his large still.

In order to add to his operation, Bob decided to reconnect with old friends from Chicago when the state of Illinois passed prohibition in 1919. He thought that the route through Kettle Falls would be a better way to ship to Chicago via the railroad at Cusson.

Bob's best chance for establishing a connection to Chicago was through Dean O'Banion, an acquaintance from many years before at McGovern's Tavern on the north side of Chicago. At that time, O'Banion was a teenager and worked at the tavern singing and serving beer. He was a small time crook when prohibition was passed in Illinois in 1919, but he soon added bootlegging to his list of criminal activities, and quickly became the leader of the Northside Gang in Chicago, which was the nemesis of the Southside Torrio and Capone Gang.

O'Banion owned a flower shop that was his front, and he provided funeral arrangements for many of the Chicago mob figures, most of whom met an early demise. O'Banion's bodyguard and best friend was a tough by the name of Louis Aterie, who was known for his hot temper and fierce loyalty to his boss.

Soon after prohibition became law in Illinois, Bob contacted O'Banion and asked him to visit Ranier. Bob was hoping that he could add him to his list of customers and establish a new pipeline to Chicago. On a hot sunny day in August of 1919, Dean O'Banion, his fiancée Viola Kaniff, and his bodyguard Louis Aterie arrived by train in Ranier. Bob met them at the station and brought them to the farmhouse for dinner.

Bob cooked the dinner himself and he and Cora entertained the group. Cora had no idea of who O'Banion was and found him to be quite charming at the dinner table. His fiancée, Viola, was beautiful and entertaining with her French accent. Aterie had little to add to the conversation, and he stayed close to O'Banion. Bob noticed the shoulder holster and gun he carried straight away. Surprisingly, O'Banion was known in Chicago for his love and respect for women. The one criminal element he refused to get involved with was prostitution and he liked the fact that Bob was a family man. It was easy to see that he was impressed with Cora, as he was adamant that she accompany them to Kettle Falls the next day.

The group headed up Rainy Lake the following morning in the *Mayflower* with Cap Thompson at the helm. Bob showed O'Banion the operation and the route through Kettle Falls.

O'Banion was known to sell good liquor and he was only interested in authentic Canadian whiskey. He and Bob made a deal that day for Bob to provide his product to O'Banion's Chicago market. Bob knew that doing business with O'Banion had its dangers, but at least he had known him from his Chicago days.

Everything was going well until the fall of 1919 when Sheriff Van Ettan and his officers raided both of Bob's restaurants. For once, Bob wasn't tipped off before the raids. He and his employees were arrested, and Bob was charged with three counts of possession of intoxicating liquors for the purpose of sale because he was the owner. Although Bob wasn't at the restaurant when they raided the place, Sheriff Van Ettan and Deputy Reedy took great pleasure in coming to the farmhouse and putting Bob under arrest. They led him out in handcuffs in front of Cora and Charlie, which upset both of them. Bob was arraigned and a date was set for the grand jury. His lawyer, Frank Palmer, had him out on bail before Van Ettan could complete the paperwork.[39]

When it came time for the trial, Bob's employees refused to testify against him, instead choosing to pay the fine and do the time. Frank Palmer acted as Bob's lawyer, and expected the

---

[39] Court Documents

charges against Bob to be eventually dropped for lack of evidence. Sheriff Van Ettan was irate when shortly after the arrest it was discovered that the evidence had been lost.

The prosecutor still refused to dismiss the charges and the case was continued so many times that Bob had still not appeared before the grand jury by January 16, 1920, when prohibition was passed on the national level. Prohibition was now the law of the land, and with it an even greater surge in the level of organized crime throughout the country.

In the spring of 1920, people in Koochiching County were worried the influenza that had spread throughout Minnesota and Koochiching County in October of 1918 was back. The "Spanish Flu" had spread all over the globe, an estimated twenty million people had died, and the north country of Minnesota was not spared. There had been over three hundred deaths in Koochiching County during the peak of the influenza season in 1918. Each year afterward, the number of cases diminished, but there were still cases being reported. There was talk of temporarily closing the soft drink parlors and public meeting places, as they had in 1918. This strain of influenza was unusual in that it seemed to affect young healthy adults the most. Many people started wearing masks again when they ventured out.

On the evening of May 6, 1920, Carrie made a frantic phone call to Bob at the hotel in Ranier, saying that Cora was very ill. Bob was surprised because she had seemed fine that morning. He rushed home to the farm and found Cora in her room lying down. When Bob saw that Cora was feverish and chilled, he ran to call Dr. Withrow to come to the house as soon as possible.

The doctor examined Cora and said that she had developed pneumonia from the influenza. Her breathing was labored and her chest ached with each breath. The doctor was surprised because the number of cases of influenza in the county had decreased dramatically; there had been very few cases in the last months.

Bob was shocked that she could become so ill so quickly, but Dr. Withrow told him that it wasn't unusual for this strain of the flu. He had done his best, but by the next day Cora had not improved.

Bob telephoned the Olsen home in Superior and spoke to Cora's stepmother, Bertha, informing her that Cora was very ill. Bertha assured him that she would tell Cora's father about her illness. Bob expected to get a telephone call or telegram from Cora's father, but none came. Throughout that day and the next, Cora's breath became more and more labored. On the evening of the second day, she opened her eyes and asked Charlie and Bob to come nearer.

She took Charlie's hand in hers and whispered, "If anything should happen to me, you are to stay with Bob. Bob will be your father from now on and he will take good care of you. I tried the best I could and I am so sorry to leave you. Bob loves you like a son, and he will adopt you. I give him my permission." Her last words were that she loved them both more than anything, and she had never been happier than when the three of them had been together. Cora passed away with Bob and Charlie at her side on May 9, 1920.[40] Carrie Shehan and Dr. Withrow witnessed Cora's last request.

Bob made the call to Superior soon after Cora passed and asked to speak to Cora's father. Cora's older brother Thomas took the call. Fighting back tears, Bob told Thomas that Cora had passed away, then asked him, "Where is Cora's father? Why didn't he call or come to see her?" Bob was seething with anger. The usually soft spoken Bob found his voice rising. The doctor answered almost apologetically. "He chose not

---

[40] Charlie Williams Outline

to come, but he does want her body taken to Eau Claire to be buried in the family plot."

"What kind of people are you?" Bob asked him, "How could he not want to see her? She was a beautiful person. We were so lucky to have her! I will never love another woman as I loved her. And what of your young nephew?! He is a wonderful boy. What of him? You people will rot in hell for how you treated them." The doctor, obviously embarrassed, answered, "She shamed our family. She married a no good drifter."

Bob responded, "Anything could have happened to them when he let them go to the frontier alone. A lot of women would have lowered themselves, but she didn't. Did you know that she worked physical labor in a saw mill to support Charlie? I saw how hard she worked to take care of her son. You didn't even know her. She was a fine woman! If you dare, tell your old man from me that he is a coward, and that I would stop him from taking her if I could. She should be buried near people who loved her." Bob noticed Charlie standing nearby and could see by the look on his face that he must have heard him. "I will leave this for now," he said under his breath, "But you haven't heard the last of me. I will care for Charlie because I love him as my son. Cora's last request was that I adopt Charlie and he stay with me. None of you deserve him anyway."

126

Bob and Charlie were both in shock. Bob tried to be strong for Charlie; the boy was devastated, and they both looked as though they had aged overnight. Carrie made them dinner, but neither of them could eat. Bob told Charlie as he was climbing in bed, "It's going to take time, son, but we will get through each day together. Try to get some sleep. I will see you in the morning." The big house was very quiet without Cora.

Bob made the arrangements for Cora's body to be shipped to Eau Claire where she was buried beside Arthur and her mother on May 15th, 1920. Her father did not purchase a headstone for her; he placed a small plaque on her grave that simply said "Olsen". At no time did he ask to see Charlie. At the house in Superior, Bertha Olsen was not speaking to her husband.

An obituary was published in the newspaper in Eau Claire, most likely by Cora's Aunt Mollie, but Cora was referred to as a "Mrs. Grant." Bob surmised that Cora's father did not want his acquaintances to know who Cora had married. According to the obituary, a small service was held at Aunt Mollie's house in Eau Claire for Cora Cecelia Olsen. Bob and Charlie were not included, and Cora was buried without ceremony or a church service.[41] Her case of influenza was one of the last reported in Koochiching County that year.

One morning a few days after Cora's death, Bob was awakened by car doors slamming in the yard. He looked out the window and saw Sheriff Van Ettan, Deputy Reedy, and several other officers. Van Ettan had a piece of paper in his hand and pounded on the back door. When Bob answered, Van Ettan pushed his way in and asked where Charlie was. Bob said that he was sleeping and Van Ettan gave the paper to Bob. It was an order from Judge Wright removing Charlie from the home and placing him in the custody of the county. Bob called his lawyer, Frank Palmer, but Palmer said that Bob would have to let the authorities take Charlie. They would file an emergency motion with the judge to try to get him back. Bob would never forget the scene that followed.

Van Ettan followed Bob up the stairs and into Charlie's room. Van Ettan woke the boy and told him to pack some things, that he was leaving to be placed with the county and that

---

[41] Obituary for Cora Cecelia Olsen in *Eau Claire Leader*

he would be sent to a foster home. Charlie told him that his mother had told him he was to stay with Bob, and that Bob was going to be his dad. Charlie begged Van Ettan to not to take him away from his dad. Bob told Charlie quietly that he would get him back as soon as he could. He told Van Ettan that he needed to talk to Charlie alone and pushed Van Ettan toward the door. Bob shut the door in Van Ettan's face and Van Ettan stood outside the door.

Bob sat Charlie down on the bed. "They are doing this because of me, not because of you. They want to get back at me, but I will figure it out." He said. "If the county will not let you come home right away, run back here the first chance you get. I will never stop trying to get you back. I am starting adoption proceedings with my lawyer. You are my son now and I love you. We both have to be strong right now. Can you do that, Son? " Tears were streaming down Charlie's face. Bob held him for a couple of minutes, and then Charlie looked up and said, "I can do it. I will see you soon. I love you, Dad." Charlie and Bob opened the door and walked past the officer. Bob said under his breath to the officer as he brushed past him, "What kind of a man hurts a child for spite? Your time will come." The officer sneered, "Is that a threat, Williams?" "I don't make threats." he answered. Carrie caught Van Ettan by the sleeve as he pulled Charlie out the door, "Shame on you for taking our Charlie. You should be careful. What goes around comes around!"

Charlie was overcome with grief. Van Ettan brought him to the county courthouse as stated in the order the judge had signed. Charlie was silent in the police car. He wanted to strike out at the officer, but he remembered what Bob had said and held his temper. He was brought to the judge's chambers and the judge explained to Charlie that he was going into foster care. Charlie tried to tell him that his mother had asked Bob to take him when she died, that they were going to get married, and that Bob was his dad now. "I'm sorry, Son, but they weren't legally married. It is the law." Van Ettan interrupted the exchange, and said that he would take Charlie to the state social worker where he would be placed with a family. "My dad will get me back, you wait and see!" Charlie said to Van Ettan. "You will be living with decent people." Van Ettan answered. Charlie asked him as he was being led away, "Like you?!"

The first family Charlie was sent to stay with was the Harry Smith family in Ranier. Harry Smith was a friend of Bob's, and they were nice people, but Charlie was terribly homesick and sad about his mother. Mabel Smith was a kind woman and had known Charlie's mother. She tried to make Charlie feel welcome, but she could see that the boy was miserable. The first night, after the family was asleep, Charlie dressed and quietly slipped out the door. He walked the mile to the farmhouse and went to bed in his room. Bob was at the breakfast table the next morning when he got up. He greeted Charlie with a simple, "Good morning, Son."

Bob filed a petition for adoption through Frank Palmer, but Palmer was not optimistic.[42] The three charges for bootlegging pending against him in county court had not yet been dismissed, although Palmer was sure the charges would be dropped for lack of evidence. The worst strike against him was that he was single and he had not married Cora. The authorities did not care that Bob was planning to marry Cora when her divorce was final. No one seemed to care that it was Cora's last wish that Charlie live with Bob. Even so, Charlie saw his dad on a regular basis and Bob tried hard to get him back.

The case was heard in October of 1920 at the Koochiching County Courthouse. Frank Keyes, mayor of the

---

[42] Adoption Petition for Charlie Keenan

Falls, and another friend, G.W. Anderson of Ranier testified on Bob's behalf. Pete Gibbons and his wife were also at the hearing to support Bob and Charlie.

Dr. M.E. Withrow testified that Charlie was in perfect health, the state of the home was excellent, and that he had witnessed Cora's last request. He stated he knew that Bob planned to give Charlie a good education and that there were lots of books and musical instruments in the house; he had a competent housekeeper who had known Charlie for years who would help care for him.

The judge heard testimony from Sheriff Hughes Van Ettan regarding Bob's bootlegging activities. Deputies H.E. Day and H. Reedy, and County Clerk J.M. Drummond, all testified that Bob did not have a good reputation in town. Palmer pointed out that Bob had never been convicted of a crime, but the comment went unnoticed.

The case worker was Florence Dann of the Children's Bureau. Miss Dann testified regarding the interview she conducted with Bob. She said she suspected he had been drinking, and that he was very nervous. She had also interviewed other people in Ranier and some of the foster parents. She wound up recommending the adoption be denied because she considered

Bob unfit to be a father. She said the good people of Ranier did not give her a favorable impression of him.

The judge let Bob make a statement. Bob told the judge that Cora had been abandoned by her husband and that she had been working as Bob's housekeeper for the last five years. He said they after several years they had fallen in love and they were going to be married once Cora's divorce was final. He said he had grown to love Charlie, that Charlie had lived at the farmhouse for the last five years, and that he had been healthy and happy. He testified that Charlie had been a good student, but his school work had suffered from being in the foster homes. He said that Cora herself asked on her death bed that Bob should be allowed to adopt Charlie and that she had given her permission. Bob affirmed that he was deeply attached to Charlie, and asked respectfully that the judge grant the petition and let Charlie come home.

In December, Judge Wright denied the petition for adoption and ordered that Charlie stay in foster care.[43] Over that year, Charlie was sent to twenty-three different foster homes in the area.[44] He spent very little time in the homes, as he would

---

[43] Notes on adoption case
[44] Charles Williams Oral History

run back to the farmhouse the first chance he got. Some of the foster parents treated him well, others did not.

The following months were a dark time for both Charlie and Bob. Losing Cora had been very hard on both of them. Bob was in a state of depression and was drinking too much. He tried to put on a good front for Charlie, but he could not hide his sadness. During the weeks after the adoption was denied, Bob spent a good part of his time alone at the farmhouse. He let his employees run his businesses and sat thinking of Cora, of the first time he saw her and the day he realized that he loved her. It was love at first sight, really, and he had never believed in that. He realized how lucky they had been to have the short time they had together, and that love like that doesn't happen to everyone. Not everyone is fortunate enough to know that special kind of happiness. He came to realize that he couldn't give up the fight for Charlie. Cora would have wanted him to keep trying to get their son back. There had to be an answer, and he would find it.

Charlie tried to understand why he wasn't able to stay at the farm with Bob, but it made no sense to him. His mother's family had never wanted him and his real father had abandoned him. Bob was the only person who cared about him, so why couldn't he live with him? He did not articulate any of these feelings; he just kept running away from the foster homes and missing school.

On a cold night in January, about a month after the adoption had been denied, Bob sat in the lobby of his hotel in Ranier drinking a whiskey and smoking a cigar. It was late in the evening, and he could see from the window that the lights were still on in Lil King's apartment, which was located at the back of her candy store just across the street.

He drained the whiskey in his glass, got up, put out the cigar, and walked across the street. He walked around to the back door of Lil's building, and just as he started up the steps, she glanced out and saw him there. Lil, clad in a dressing gown, opened the door and walked down the steps to meet him. She took his hand and led him up the steps and inside.

Bob began to spend more time with Lil. They had always enjoyed each other's company, but now they were more than friends.

In the spring of 1921, almost a year after Cora's death, Bob thought of a way to remedy the situation with Charlie and to get him back at home. Bob had come out of his depression and was trying to think of a way to save the boy, who he had promised to raise as his own. He sat Charlie down one day and asked him what he thought about Bob getting married. He said that the judge might change his mind if he was married. He told Charlie that he was going to ask the lady at the candy store, Lil King,[45] to marry him, if Charlie would go along with it. Charlie knew Lil from the confectionary store in Ranier; he often bought candy there with the other Ranier kids. He thought she was a nice lady and very pretty.

Bob went on to say that Lil was a smart businesswoman, and she could help Bob because he was having a hard time operating all of his businesses on his own. He had purchased more real estate properties along the beach road, things were getting more complicated, and he needed help from someone he could trust. Bob said that Lil had been a good friend to him after Cora died, that he had grown to love her, and that she would be a good mother to Charlie. Charlie thought about how great it

[45] Ranier 1920 Census

would be to be home again, and he agreed that Bob should marry Lil.[46]

The next day, Bob visited Lil at the store and asked if they could talk. They walked down to the harbor and sat on the bench near Duluth Street Landing. "I know that this isn't the most romantic proposal, but I do love you, Lil. You have helped me so much this year. You would do me an honor if you would be my wife, and you would be helping me to get my son back. I only ask that you try to love him as your own. It may take time, but he is a great kid." "Well," she answered, "I know he is a good kid. It won't be hard to love him, but I am new to it and I will have a lot to learn about being a mother. I know I'm not your first love, and you aren't mine, but I think we make a good pair. We have fun together, and I agree that you would be lucky to have me. We are also going to make a lot of money." Bob laughed and agreed wholeheartedly. At that point he retrieved a small velvet box from his pocket. Inside was a flawless one carat diamond solitaire. They were married by Judge Wright in May of 1921 at the courthouse, almost a year to the day after Cora died. Harry and Mabel Smith stood up for them and Charlie was there with Frank Palmer.

---

[46] Charlie Williams Outline

Soon after, Lil sold her candy business in Ranier and moved to the farmhouse. It took a few weeks, but the authorities finally allowed Charlie to go home. It was at this time that he took the name Charles Williams. There was a surprise for Charlie the day he was allowed to go home to the farmhouse. Bob and Lil had dinner and cake for Charlie and presented him with a Corgi puppy who he named Buster. Charlie went to bed happily that night knowing that he could stay at home and sleep in his own bed, and that he had his very own dog for the first time in his life.

Sheriff Van Ettan continued his zealous pursuit of the bootleggers and smugglers. His many arrests were heralded in the newspapers, and he was immune to the bribery that some of the officers succumbed to. No one doubted his bravery, but he was a hard man with a quick temper. He took pride in being physically fit and he had no problem with hurting someone in the course of an arrest. He was serious in character and not prone to laughter. It didn't help that the sheriff lived with the fact that despite his best efforts, the person he knew to be responsible for most of the bootlegging and smuggling in the area remained a free man.

As a businessman, Bob considered the occasional confiscation of his liquor, the fines and attorney's fees he paid for his men, the money he gave their families during their incarceration, and the bribes he paid to the authorities to be a part of doing business. He didn't take any of it personally and he didn't want anyone to get hurt. In any case, the authorities stopped but a drop in the bucket of the alcohol that was moving across the border. He did regret was that he could no longer be close friends with Jess Rose. They had gradually grown apart after Bob had begun bootlegging. It seemed that neither of the men could keep up the pretense.

One incident showed the people of Ranier and the Falls just how serious Van Ettan and Reedy were about catching the bootleggers, and depths they would go to in order to make an arrest.

On April 25, 1922, the *Daily Journal* reported regarding the fate of a smuggler named John McCochran: "John McCochran of Fort Frances is in a hospital at International Falls, fatally wounded. He is alleged to have been shot accidentally by

Hugh Reedy, deputy sheriff, while McCochran and a confederate, Charles Gillis, were attempting to evade arrest on a charge of smuggling liquor. Although McCochran was shot while fleeing arrest, Sheriff Van Ettan and his deputy, Hugh Reedy, who fired the fatal shot, insist the wounded man was hit accidentally. Sunday night, McCochran paddling a boat loaded with several cases of whisky crossed the river from Fort Frances, Canada, to International Falls, American side, according to the officials.

The rum runner was met on the river bank by Charles Gillis, taxi driver, who helped McCochran load the liquor into a waiting auto. When the transfer was complete Van Ettan and Reedy sprang from a place of concealment and placed the rower and the taxi driver under arrest. But before they could shackle their prisoners McCochran leaped into the boat and was swallowed up in the darkness as he rowed across the river. Reedy fired once in the direction of the boat, "just to scare" McCochran, he declares.

This morning McCochran's body, with a bullet wound through the abdomen, was found on a log boom on the Fort Frances side of the river. He is unconscious and, surgeons say, has small chance of recovery. Officials believe Reedy's bullet ricocheted from the water and tore into the fleeing boatman, who managed to reach the Canadian bank before collapsing upon the boom. No arrests have been made in connection with the shooting, although Gillis is in custody on a smuggling charge."

Many people living in the area questioned whether the shooting had been an accident. Sheriff Van Ettan and Deputy Reedy were feared and despised by many. It was considered an act of cowardice to shoot a man in the back, especially over a few bottles of whiskey. Bob had no love for Van Ettan, and now he knew what the sheriff and his men were capable of, and that they had no qualms about killing. Bob always made sure he had his pearl handled pistol nearby, and told his men that under no circumstance were they to try to run from Van Ettan if caught.

Bob's pistol   Courtesy of KCHS

Another incident of violence occurred in Bob's restaurant in Ranier, and was reported in the *Duluth News Tribune* in December of 1922. "One man was killed, another mortally wounded and the soft drink place where the tragedy occurred robbed by James Conroy, alias McDonald, age 35, at 7 a.m. at Ranier, a small town near here today. Conroy after taking shelter in the woods was captured by Deputy Hugh Reedy. Conroy is held without charge. He will be formally charged with murder tomorrow." Frank Jevne, country attorney said.

Pat Finnegan, age fifty, a customer in the place, died instantly from a bullet wound in the left lung. The gun flourished by Conroy, apparently without provocation and with robbery a probable motive was a Colt 45.

After killing Finnegan, Conroy turned the gun on James Lessard, age 32, a bartender of the place. Lessard was hit twice in the chest and was sent to the Northern Minnesota hospital, with hope for his recovery abandoned. At the hospital, he identified Conroy as the man who shot him and Finnegan. Frightened by the gunman, Bert Lessard, another inmate of the place, and a brother of the wounded man, scurried through the door. He was made the target of two shots that missed him.

Two cash registers were rifled by Conroy after the shooting. He was trailed for two miles in the woods by Deputy Reedy, who was compelled to use his flashlight. Unaided, Reedy placed Conroy under arrest. His gun, containing one loaded bullet, was taken from him and $300 cash. Conroy refuses to talk and did not intimate what prompted his action. James Lessard, in a statement reported that Conroy entered the place and recklessly brandished his gun. "Here, you better put that away, you might hurt someone." Lessard said Finnegan cautioned Conroy. To which Conroy replied, "Maybe you want some of this yourself," then fired.[47]

Bob knew Pat Finnegan and the Lessard brothers well. Pat Finnegan was a congenial man and well-liked by the people of Ranier. Bob had been friends with the Lessard family since his move to Ranier and the Lessard brothers had worked for him for years. The Lessard brothers were the most congenial men Bob had ever encountered. All of them were jolly men, with big laughs. They looked so much alike that some people had trouble telling them apart. Bob worried about them and all of the men who worked for him. The violence seemed to be escalating in the area. It was clear to Bob that the prohibition of alcohol had

---

[47] *Duluth News Tribune*

not abated any of it, and in fact, there was more violence than ever before. It seemed that all prohibition had accomplished was to needlessly make criminals out of him and many others. The money he used to pay for liquor licenses now went to pay-offs to the officials. In with the new law, out went the old laws that regulated liquor. There had been many deaths in the county due to bad moonshine or poisonous homebrew made in the blind pigs.

Within months of the Finnegan murder, the residents of Ranier were shocked to hear that Sheriff Hughes Van Ettan and Falls Patrolman Wilber McMicken had both been killed when they had gone to arrest two local men, Joe Bosnon and John Nigro, for passing forged checks. The newspaper reported that the officers were accompanied by William Carpenter, who had reported the crime to Van Ettan, saying that Carpenter led the officers to the hideout, a small shack near the railroad tracks on the east side of the Falls. When the officers ordered the men to come out and surrender, they failed to comply. When one of the officers tried to force the door with a heavy plank, one of the fugitives fired through the door with a large caliber rifle, hit-ting both Van Ettan and McMicken and causing a great loss of blood.

William Carpenter went for help and the two officers were brought to the hospital where they were both pronounced dead. The next morning, Deputy Hugh Reedy organized a large posse and a manhunt was staged to arrest Bosnon and Nigro. Bosnon was located in a wooded section in the south part of the Falls and was shot and killed when he fired at officers. Nigro was located at Ericsberg the following day and surrendered.[48]

There was talk that the officers had been set up, as Van Ettan was not well liked by much of the population and hated by the bootleggers. Bob disagreed, and he wasn't surprised to hear the news. Van Ettan was dealing with dangerous people on a daily basis. Bob suspected that the men in the shack were crazy on bad moonshine when they shot the officers. There had been several such shootings around the county, one particularly bad one in Loman, when four people were shot in a blind big by a man gone crazy on bad moonshine. The violence was increasing, and Van Ettan and his men had recently been the ones to escalate the violence by shooting a man in the back. Van Ettan was as tough as they came, but Bob had known that even his luck would run out sooner or later.

---

[48] *Duluth News Tribune*

By the time Judge Wright allowed Charlie to go home, he wasn't the same happy-go-lucky boy he had been. The trauma of his mother's death and being sent from foster home to foster home had taken its toll. Charlie had gone from being a good student to hardly attending school. He fell so far behind in his studies that he was forced to repeat a grade in school, which only added to his depression and feelings of isolation. He consoled himself with his new puppy and tried to look on the bright side, but he still missed his mother and it was hard to overcome the feeling of sadness that would overcome him at times.

Charlie didn't understand why his mother's family had not wanted to see him. He was baffled by the fact they hadn't come to see his mother when she was dying. Why was his grandfather so mean? His mother hadn't told him much about his real dad, other than his name and that he had left them before he was born. Once, he had heard his mother telling Bob that his real dad had gone to Canada and that he had relatives in the Falls, but that they had denied their kinship. Charlie had a lot of questions that only his mother could have answered. He wondered who he was and where he came from, and there was no one to

147

help him figure it out.[49] He was grateful to Bob for not giving up on him and he appreciated Lil's kindness to him. He decided to try harder in school in order to make Bob and Lil proud of him.

Some of the people in Ranier treated Charlie differently after Cora died and Bob married Lil; a few of his childhood friends were no longer allowed to see him. On several occasions, his temper got the best of him and he wound up getting into fights with boys who teased him. Luckily, his best friends, Scottie and Paul Couture, John Bishop, Jack Green, and Sylvester Keyes, had been there for him through it all, and they remained his best friends.

---

[49] Charlie Williams Outline

Kettle Falls Dock   circa 1918   Courtesy of KCHS

The bright spot in all of this was that Charlie was allowed to spend his summers at Kettle Falls. Since Lil married Bob and sold her building and candy business in Ranier to the Victor Davis family, she spent her summers running the hotel at Kettle Falls. Charlie was happy to go with her. Bob was there for most of the summer, but spent some of his time running the businesses in Ranier. Charlie seemed to forget all of the bad things that had happened to him when he was at Kettle Falls. He felt close to his mother at Kettle Falls because they had shared so many good times there. It also helped that his dear friend Carrie Shehan went with Lil to the hotel to work in the summer.

Charlie made friends with the sons of the Native Americans that traded at the Kettle Falls trading posts, spent many hours canoeing and learning his way on the big lake, berry-picking, and learning how to fish and hunt. Charlie developed a love and respect for the Native American people that would endure all of his life. With each summer, he became more familiar with the big lake, with the many bays and islands and the people who lived there.

Lil was good to him and he liked her very much. Lil had a great sense of humor and made Charlie laugh. She made sure that he was well taken care of, but she wasn't his mother and she was not the most affectionate person. Charlie knew that she cared about him, and that she was busy running the hotel and cooking for the loggers and commercial fisherman who came to stay there. Although Lil was a good cook in her own right and a good baker, Bob taught her to cook all of his specialty dishes that were served at the hotel. The lumberjacks and commercial fishermen loved to eat there, but Lil was tough on them. She made them carry their own dishes to the kitchen after every meal and some of them could be seen washing dishes or peeling potatoes.

The men also loved to drink and dance in the bar room. The nickelodeon that sat in the corner had a painting of a nude dance hall girl hanging above it. There were pictures of Gibson girls and dancehall girls on the walls, and the men danced with "girls" to the lively music from the nickelodeon. The floor of the bar room was starting to show the wear of the loggers' dancing, small marks covered the floor, made by the cleats on the bottom of the big hobnail boots they wore. A barrel stove sat in a corner with a pile of wood beside it. A back room was designed to hide liquor within its walls. A sign hung above the till that said, "An honest bartender is worth his weight in gold."

Most of the women who plied their trade with the loggers and fishermen lived in tents or small cabins in close proximity to the hotel during the summer months. A few of them who could afford it rented a room in the hotel. Some of them had colorful names, like Lumberjack Carrie, Yellow Rose, and Big Belle. The ladies would return to their houses or the shanty town in Ranier at the end of the season and spend the winter there. Whenever any of the ladies saw Charlie, they would call out hello to him. They teased him and told him that he was very good looking and asked him to come to visit when he got older. They gave him money to run errands for them and treated him with kindness. They all paid Buster a lot of attention and gave him treats.

Charlie was left to his own devices each summer and explored the woods around the hotel and Rainy Lake extensively. Kettle Falls was a very fun and interesting place for a boy to be. Charlie spent time with Oscar Nelson, a trapper who lived in a log cabin on the Namakan side of the portage; Oscar was a great friend of Lil's and watched out for Charlie while he was at Kettle Falls. Oscar was a long and tall man, with large hands and a handle-bar mustache. He was a quiet, kindly man, and he loved to tell stories. Oscar trapped game in the winter and did odd jobs at the hotel in the summer. He made a large chair out of logs that sat on the front porch of the hotel. He was often seen sitting in his chair, smoking his pipe.

One of the most interesting characters at Kettle Falls was a man by the name of Burt Upton. He was called Catamaran by the locals because he had arrived at Kettle Falls on a catamaran that he had built himself and sailed across Crane and Namakan lakes. It was said that he may have been running from the law. He was mysterious, as no one knew where he had come from, although he had a British accent and claimed to have been a teacher in his former life. He lived in a cave on an island a short distance from Kettle Falls and planted flower and vegetable gardens all around his camp. He always seemed to have money, which puzzled the locals because he dressed in rags and rarely bathed.

Charlie enjoyed his time at Kettle Falls, and as each perfect summer came to an end, he dreaded the trip down Rainy Lake and going back to school. Buster seemed to understand. He snuggled next to Charlie in the bow of the *Mayflower* all the way down the big lake.

Ranier School House circa 1909   Courtesy of KCHS

Charlie attended the two story schoolhouse in Ranier until the fall of 1924 when he was sixteen years old. That fall, the school district opened a big new high school in the Falls and all of the teenagers of the area where required to attend. The new school was located on Sixth Avenue across the street from the court house on Fourth Street. It had taken three years to build the large square building at a cost of $300,000. Over three hundred students attended from the Falls and the surrounding area on the day the school opened.

The roads had been sparse at the beginning of the settlement of Koochiching County and most of the ten

154

Koochiching townships had a one room school house. By the early 1920s there were a great number of those small schoolhouses scattered about the county. With the improved road system, the school officials started to abandon the one room schoolhouses in favor of building bigger schools in the towns with bigger populations. Other small high schools had been built in the nearby towns of Big Falls, Indus, Littlefork, and Northome.[50]

Charlie was doing better in school now that he was back living with Bob and Lil, but he was still behind a year in his studies, which bothered him a lot. Sylvester Keyes, Paul Couture, and Charlie had always been in the same grade before his mother's death. Charlie still considered it unfair they had set him back and he wasn't excited when fall came and school started for the year.

Charlie and the other students of high school age from Ranier and the areas east as far as Jackfish Bay rode a bus to the new high school. The bus started in the morning by picking up the students at Jespersen's dairy farm at Jackfish Bay, which was at the end of the lake road and six miles east of the Falls. The bus then turned around and picked up the students along the

---

[50] *Taming the Wilderness* by Hiram Drache

way to Ranier and the Falls. Charlie boarded the bus in front of the farmhouse by the beach on Sand Bay, and the Ranier kids boarded the bus at the bank building on the corner of Spruce and Duluth streets.

That first morning, everyone on the bus was nervous about going to the new high school. The students from Ranier and up the lake didn't know what to expect when they got off the bus, some feared they would be made fun of for their lack of sophistication. A few of the Falls kids were aware that Charlie's dad was in the liquor business, and someone said the word "bootlegger" as Charlie got off the bus. Charlie heard the remark, but he decided to shrug it off. He wanted to start fresh that day, so he ignored the taunt.

Charlie had grown to almost six feet by the time he was sixteen, and he was very lean and strong like his mother; he wasn't aware that some of the girls had crushes on him. Life at the new school was hard at first for the lake kids, but most of them adapted and wound up doing well in school. Charlie did his best to ignore the teasing, but sometimes his hot temper got the best of him. It didn't take long for the teasing to stop, for no one wanted to fight Charlie Williams.[51]

---

[51] Blanche Jespersen Williams Oral History

Things changed with Sheriff Van Ettan's death and most of the authorities were more lax in their effort to catch the bootleggers. Deputy Reedy had been elected sheriff, but his boss's death seemed to take some of the wind out of his sails. He would not succumb to bribery, but he was not as avid to catch the bootleggers. He did his job and tried to protect the citizens of Koochiching County.

Many others did succumb to bribery and local law enforcement began to look the other way. Jess Rose was now the head customs officer at Ranier and continued to show due diligence in his duties. He caught many people at the Ranier Depot as they tried to smuggle Canadian whiskey in their bags or by other means. Bob tried his best to keep his bootlegging activities away from the railroad in Ranier, instead opting to smuggle by boat through Kettle Falls. During the winter, his men often snuck whiskey across Sand Bay from Canada by sleigh, and then onto the railroad south of Ranier, after the boxcars had been inspected at the depot.

Billy Noonan, the editor of the *Baudette Region*, made the observation that, "Prohibition along the border had been a great success, aside from the fact that there was more drinking than ever before."

Bob's operation proved the point, as his business had grown by leaps and bounds since federal prohibition had been passed. People weren't about to stop drinking just because it was illegal. Since shipping liquor was legal again in Ontario, Bob continued to smuggle most of his liquor to Chicago by boat through Kettle Falls, Namakan Lake, and Crane Lake, to meet the train at Cusson, Minnesota, and by plane, to St. Louis, St. Paul, and Kansas City.

Bob chuckled when the *Falls Daily Press* reported, "Winging its way through the darkness, guided solely by the dim lights of the small towns over which it passes and at sufficient altitude to reduce engine noise to a minimum, a mysterious aircraft is operating from a place a few miles south of Winnipeg to a destination in the United States. It is believed that the airplane is the link between an international gang of bootleggers operating in both countries."

Although he was doing well eluding the authorities, things didn't always go as planned for Bob. The federal agents were constantly watching him. One of the prohibition agents, Officer Bradley, lived near Ranier. Bob's men constantly monitored his whereabouts. Three of Bob's men were arrested by the federal officer in 1924 when Bradley caught them smuggling liquor by boat across the border near Ranier. They were met by the "feds" at the Ranier dock as they attempted landing a boat filled with kegs of whiskey. Bob was charged along with his men. Officer Bradley arrested Bob at the restaurant, even found his pistol and confiscated it.

The authorities were disappointed when all three of Bob's men again refused to testify against him, which led to the charges being dropped against him. They were convicted in a trial in Duluth before the federal court and sent to Leavenworth Prison for three years. Bob provided support to their families, and when the men were released from prison three years later, they all returned to Ranier and continued to work for Bob smuggling booze through Canada. By that time, Officer Bradley was accepting bribes to look the other way. Shortly before Bob's men were released from Leavenworth, Officer Bradley was charged and convicted of accepting bribes. The same could not be said of Jess Rose, who continued to do his best to arrest all smugglers at the Ranier railroad crossing.

Earlier in 1924 Bob heard the news that Dean O'Banion had been murdered in his flower shop by Al Capone and his Chicago Southside Gang. Aterie was still O'Banion's body-guard, but he had overslept and had not yet shown up for work

159

on the morning Capone and his men burst into the shop, killing O'Banion with a sub-machine gun.

George "Bugs" Moran was now the head of the Northside Gang. Moran made a trip to Ranier to visit Bob and look at the operation on Rainy Lake. Bob was nervous about dealing with him because he had heard that Moran's behavior was erratic and that he could be ruthless. He was careful to be very fair and open in his business dealings with Moran. Surprisingly, Moran turned out to be congenial and pleasant to work with, although Bob had no illusions about what he was capable of. Moran seemed to enjoy the beautiful scenery and got a kick when the *Mayflower* outran a federal cruiser on the way up the big lake to Kettle Falls. Moran drank in the bar at the hotel and sang Irish songs. He took a liking to Lil, which made Bob nervous, but in the end he had acted like a gentleman in his business dealings. They dropped Moran off at the train depot in Ranier and both sighed with relief to see him go. Bob continued to ship liquor to Moran through the Kettle Falls connection.

The connections Bob made in St. Paul, Minnesota, St. Louis, and Kansas City, Missouri, were a constant source of concern. All three were "open towns", which meant that the prohibition laws were not enforced and the towns were run by local gangsters and corrupt politicians. Bob refused to go to St. Louis because of the many gangs that were always at war. He wasn't sure who would meet the plane when it landed and he worried about his pilot and plane. Bob always had Dutch land well outside of the St. Louis city limits when he delivered Bob's whiskey and only after Bob was assured of Dutch's safety.

In St. Paul, Hogan's Irish gang had complete control of the streets, so it was safer to go there. Bob and Lil both enjoyed staying at the beautiful St. Paul Hotel and occasionally went there to get away. Dutch would fly them to the St. Paul airport, where they would catch a taxi to the center of town. They ate in the best restaurants and frequented the finest clubs. Lil shopped at the many boutiques on the cobbled streets of downtown St. Paul.

They visited Chicago to attend the National Air Show and always stayed at the Palmer, where Bob still had friends.

The highlight of the year 1927 was their trip to Europe in July and August.[52] After spending a week in New York City seeing the sights, Bob and Lil sailed on the Aquitania, which was known as "The Ship Beautiful." They toured the capitols of Europe and visited Lil's sister in Sweden. They sailed back from South Hampton and entered New York Harbor on August 19th.

---

[52] Ancestry.com Passenger Information

Charlie spent the time they were away at Kettle Falls in the capable hands of Oscar Nelson and Carrie Shehan. Bob and Lil scheduled their return voyage to coincide with Charlie's return to Ranier and to school as a senior in high school.

Charlie had a wonderful summer at Kettle Falls while Bob and Lil were traveling, and although he did not look forward to going back to school, he was happy to see them upon his return to Ranier. One morning a few days after school started that fall, Charlie got off the school bus with the other Ranier students to see Blanche Jespersen, one of the lake girls, being teased by a bully. Charlie took the boy's arm, gave him a little shove, and said, "Leave her alone if you know what's good for you." The boy backed off, but as he walked away, he said under his breath, "bootlegger."

Charlie was thinking of going after him, when the school principal grabbed him by the elbow and ushered him to his office. He asked Charlie, "Why are you always causing trouble?" Charlie didn't answer. "I have no choice but to call your father, Charlie. You really have to work on controlling that temper.

Now go back to class." Charlie knew he would get a lecture when he returned home. Later that morning, as he was climbing the stairs at the school, he accidentally bumped into a girl from town. She dropped her books, and when Charlie tried to apologize and began to help her pick them up, the girl called him a dirty bootlegger's son.

That was the last straw for Charlie. He left school, and when he got home to Ranier, he told his dad that he was quitting school and that he wanted to start working for him running liquor. Bob knew that Charlie was having a hard time at school, but he refused to allow Charlie to quit school or to start bootlegging. He had promised Cora that he would help Charlie to get an education and it was very important to him that he do so. Most important, he did not want Charlie to get in trouble with the law. It was their first real argument, and Charlie was very angry, saying "Well, I'm not going back there!"

As he lay in his bed that night, Charlie thought of his options. He had heard and read about the hoboes that rode the rails across the country to find work. Charlie's favorite writer was Jack London. He had learned a lot about riding the rails in his tattered copy of London's book "The Road." Charlie decided to ride the rails to the west coast and try to find work in the shipyards. He would leave town and try to build a life far from Ranier where nobody knew him.

Charlie packed his duffle bag with the book, a couple changes of clothes, some soap and a towel, a razor, a pocket knife, stick matches, candles, can opener, some canned peaches, a blanket, and his canteen filled with water. He made sandwiches to last him a couple of days. He would bring a warm jacket, hat and gloves. He put his money in the bottom of his boots except for a few dollars. He had saved thirty dollars from doing odd jobs around the farm, and he figured it was plenty of money to last until he made it to the west coast and found a job. For protection, he took a small billy club of Bob's and tucked it inside his coat.

Charlie left his dad and Lil a letter telling them of his plans and that he was sorry for losing his temper, but that he could not stand another day of school in the Falls. He asked that they take good care of Buster and said that he would be back someday. He said he would write when he could. Charlie knew that Bob would be very hurt by his leaving, but he figured Bob was probably better off without him.

Late that evening, Charlie set off along the railroad tracks leading south out of Ranier. He would walk ahead of the train and jump on as it left the station for Duluth. From Duluth, he planned to head west across Minnesota and the prairies. He hoped he could elude the railway bulls and have an uneventful trip across country. At least he had enough money to pay for food as he went, so he wouldn't have to beg at houses along the way. He hoped he would meet people that would help him learn the ways of the hoboes. For now, he would find an open boxcar and see where it took him.

When the train came slowly by on its way out of the Ranier station, Charlie ran out of the ditch and jumped up into an open boxcar. He was surprised to see someone jump on behind him. The boy must have been hiding in the woods. He appeared to be about Charlie's age, but was smaller and looked like he could use a good meal.

Charlie introduced himself and asked the boy where he was going. "I'm Johnny Johnson and I'm going south to Duluth for now. How about you?" Charlie and Johnny hit it off right away and talked all the way to Duluth while they watched the northern lights through the door of the Pullman boxcar.

165

Johnny was on a trip across the country to find work. He had red hair and freckles and a talent for telling stories about riding the rails. He was born on the Iron Range and was twelve years old when his parents both died of the influenza. Johnny took to the rails instead of going into the care of the county. Since then, he had travelled all over the United States and Canada. The year before, Johnny had been stuck in Winnipeg for the last part of the winter. It had been an especially cold and hard winter, and he didn't wish to repeat it. He was happy to be headed south. That night, while talking and sharing Charlie's sandwiches and canned peaches, the boys decided to travel west together.

They both fell asleep and woke when the train slowed down in Duluth. Johnny showed Charlie how to get off of the train without getting hurt or getting caught by the bulls or railroad cops. The boys talked around the camp fire into the night about the route they would take, and where they could find work on the west coast. The next morning in Duluth, they jumped another freight train headed west. They hit the South Dakota border by that night.[53]

---

[53] Charlie Williams Oral History

Bob was upset that Charlie had run away. He felt that he had handled the whole thing badly and that the boy had not yet recovered from his mother's death. Charlie had promised to write though, and Bob knew that the kid could take care of himself. He prayed that he would come back safely.

Blanche Jespersen had been helping with the chores on her father's dairy farm since they had purchased the place when she was seven years old, so it was no surprise that she turned out to be a hard worker. Blanche was in the middle of her chores, which included pitching hay to the dairy cattle in the barn, and she was thinking of Charlie Williams.

Jespersen's farm was located on Jackfish Bay at the end of the highway that angled west along Rainy Lake past Crystal Beach and Point'O Pines, all the way to Ranier and the Falls. As the oldest child in the family, Blanche was the first to go to high school, and she was the first student to board the bus each morning at the end of her drive.

The Larsen family lived down the road from the Jespersen family, and Arvid and Helen Larsen were the next students to board the bus each morning. They were close to Blanche in age and had been her good friends since Blanche's family had moved to Jackfish Bay. The bus continued down the winding lake road and picked up all the teenagers on the way to the big new school in the Falls. The younger children in the neighborhood attended the Lake Park School, which was located on the Lindstrom Road, not far from Jespersen's farm.

Blanche was fortunate in that she already had a good friend at the new high school. Blanche had met Muriel Johnson years earlier when her father, Andy Jespersen, brought Blanche to town with him to pick up farm supplies. Muriel's father owned one of the hardware stores in town and Muriel was often in the store when Blanche and her father came in. Muriel was very accomplished and even had her own piano, but her intelligence and sweet personality are what drew her to Blanche. The two girls became good friends.

Blanche rested on the pitchfork as she took a break from her chores in the barn. She would have to tell Muriel what had happened at the bus stop that morning. Charlie Williams had defended her when one of the boys from town had teased her. She knew that Charlie thought she was just a kid, if he had noticed her at all, but she still thought he was the most interesting boy at school, and definitely the most handsome.

A few years before, she had heard her parents talk about Charlie's mother dying of the influenza, and that he had been taken away from his dad because his dad was a bootlegger. Blanche felt sorry for Charlie about losing his mother. She felt fortunate to have a loving mother herself. Blanche could have easily been in the same situation, because Blanche, her mother, and her brother Harold had all had the influenza in 1918, the

169

worst year. Dr. Mary Ghostley had nursed the family through it and they had all survived. She shuddered to think what would have become of her if she had lost her mother. Blanche's father, Andy Jespersen, was also sympathetic, and didn't think Bob Williams was a bad man, but he said he wasn't surprised that they had taken Charlie away. He went on to say that their neighbor Mr. Lindstrom had gotten in trouble for making moonshine, and that he suspected Bob Williams had something to do with it. Andy had also heard rumors that Bob Williams was in business with some dangerous people from Chicago.

Andy had known Bob Williams for many years, since Bob opened his restaurant in the Dutch Room. After Bob moved to Ranier, Andy Jespersen and his best friend, Jim Ewald, a farmer whose farm was located south of the Falls, would occasionally stop at the Brennan's Saloon and have a beer together. Now that prohibition was in effect, Andy didn't see Bob very often.

Blanche heard them say that Charlie's father had married Lil King, the lady who owned the candy store in Ranier, a year after Charlie's mother died. Charlie was back at the big farmhouse at the beach and the bus picked him up for school there every morning. Until that morning, Charlie had never acknowledged Blanche. She wondered what he would have to

170

say to her the next time she saw him, or if he would talk to her. She was disappointed the next day when Charlie did not get on the bus when it stopped at the beach by his father's house. A few days later, someone said that Charlie had run away from home after getting in trouble at school. Blanche felt sad and a little mad at him.

Charlie Williams at eighteen years old

Blanche was a strong and independent young woman and she came by these traits honestly. Her great-grandmother, Christina Hoard, was a widow who had immigrated to America from Sweden with her seven children. She settled in southern Minnesota in the 1860s near Kokato, Minnesota. In 1890, her eldest son, John Hoard, married Anna Linsten, a widow with two children, Victor and Hilldegard. The couple soon had two more children, Adolph, and Huldah, who was Blanche's mother. John Hoard died suddenly in Kokato in 1902. He left his wife Anna the lumber and materials to build a new house there, as it had been his plan to build the house himself.[54]

Instead of building the new house, Anna Hoard sold the building materials and used the money to set out with her four children to homestead on the Canadian border in northern Minnesota. With some other families of Swedish heritage, they homesteaded in Loman, Minnesota, in the year 1903. Their homestead sat on the west bank of the Black River, where the Black runs into the Rainy River, eleven miles downstream from Koochiching, Minnesota. It was a hard life and the family would

---

[54] Hoard Family History

come close to starving, but they survived the hardships with the help of their neighbors.

Huldah Hoard met Andy Jespersen in Loman when she was nineteen years old. Andy had emigrated from Jutland, Denmark in 1900. He spent some time in Minneapolis before heading north to settle in Loman. The petite Huldah fell in love with the handsome Dane, and the couple married in Loman in November of 1911. Blanche was born in a log cabin on their homestead on the outskirts of Loman on the bank of the Rainy River in October of 1912.

Blanche was the first born and very close to her mother. Huldah Jespersen had the scare of her life when Blanche was two years old and Dr. Mary Ghostley discovered that Blanche had been blinded in her right eye. The doctor wasn't sure whether Blanche was born with the condition, or whether she had suffered an accident of some sort. The doctor was certain that the eye should be removed and informed the Jespersens that she had scheduled Blanche for surgery in Minneapolis. The Jespersens did not have the means to travel to Minneapolis, so the kindly Dr. Mary took Blanche by train to the hospital, three hundred miles south of the border, where to everyone's delight, doctors announced that the surgery would not be necessary.

When Huldah and Andy Jespersen met the train from Minneapolis in the Falls at the appointed time, they expected the worst. They held hands while the train pulled into the station, and when Blanche emerged from the train with both of her beautiful blue eyes, the couple was overcome.

A few years after the Hoard family homesteaded in Loman, Huldah's older sister Hilldegard married a fellow homesteader named Ernest Helmer. The couple had six daughters during the first ten years of their marriage, and three of the girls, Dorothy, Florence, and Ercil were close to Blanche's age and her close friends throughout her childhood. The Helmer family suffered extreme hardship after Uncle Ernie lost his hand in a farm accident. Ernie overcame the handicap and became more than proficient with his "hook" and continued farming at Loman. He was a hard worker and was one of the few farmers in the area that had modern farm equipment.

In August of 1909 Huldah's oldest brother, Vic Linsten, married a girl named Mabel McComb. The couple had several children between 1910 and 1920. Vic became the deputy sheriff assigned to Loman and the surrounding area. He was a kind man and Huldah adored him. Vic did his best to keep the town of Loman liquor free upon the passage of the county option law. Throughout prohibition, Loman remained a peaceful and law abiding community for the most part, unlike Ranier and the Falls. This was largely due to the diligence of Deputy Vic Linsten.

The Paul Earley and James Ewald families had been great friends with the Jespersen family since their days in Loman. Both families owned farms on the outskirts of the Falls. There was always work to be done on the farms and the families often helped each other with plowing and planting in the spring, barn raisings, and "putting up hay" each fall. There were monthly card games and birthday gatherings when all would attend. Blanche, Harold, Margaret, and their baby brother, Wayne, had many cousins and friends come to visit while growing up on the farm in Jackfish Bay. Margaret Earley and her sisters, and Chris and Woodrow Ewald were some of Blanche's first childhood friends, mainly because the mothers, Mrs. Jespersen, Mrs. Ewald and Mrs. Earley were the best of friends. The three women were well known for their wonderful baked goods. Mrs. Ewald's sugar cookies were a favorite, as were Mrs. Jespersen's ginger cookies and Swedish rye bread. Mrs. Earley made the best pies and apple dumplings. All three women were excellent cooks and served specialty dishes from the old countries. The families saw each other through highs and lows through the years.

When Blanche was three years old, the family moved from Loman to the Falls and Andy Jespersen worked in the paper mill. Her brother Harold and sister Margaret were born in a small house on Sixth Street. In the spring of 1920, the family moved six miles east to the farm on Jackfish Bay, where Blanche's youngest brother, Wayne, was born.

The Jespersens purchased the farm and twenty-four head of dairy cattle from Algot Erickson, who had homesteaded there. After moving to the farm, they made friends with their new neighbors, the Larsen, Lindstrom, Weberg, Christenson, Johnson, and Anderson families. Huldah Jespersen's sweet disposition made her a favorite with the neighbors. Andy Jespersen was a good man, a hard worker, and always willing to help his neighbors.

In July of 1920 the Koochiching County School Board had voted to purchase a portable one room school house for the Jackfish Bay area that would be known as the Lake Park School. The school house was made by the American Portable House Company at a cost of $1248.00. All of the neighborhood children were required to attend Lake Park School, which was located on the Lindstrom Road about a half a mile from the Jespersen farm. The Jespersen family, along with their neighbors, helped to prepare the building site by clearing timber from the land and by helping to dig a well.

The school opened in the fall of 1920 with about twenty-four students from the ages of five to fourteen. Blanche loved going to school there as did all of her friends in the neighborhood. The teachers boarded with the neighborhood families as was the custom at the time.[55]

The neighborhood children walked to school when the weather permitted, and traveled by horse and sleigh during the winter, when the temperature could drop to forty degrees below zero or lower. The teachers at the Lake Park School were well loved by the students and their parents. The teachers not only taught school, but were responsible for the chores at the school, which included gathering fire wood, cleaning, shoveling snow, and carrying water from the well. The children often helped with the chores and didn't consider it punishment.

The school was also the location for social gatherings throughout the year. There were many parties and holiday cele-

---

[55] *Lake Park School*, by Helen Larsen Trask.

brations, plays and programs, and the little school house was always beautifully decorated. There were many happy times at the Lake Park School during the seven years of its existence.

Mrs. McPeek from Birch Point Resort often invited the children of the neighborhood to visit. She built the cabins at her resort with the help of one of the Jackfish Bay settlers, Pete Anderson, who owned a saw mill on the Lindstrom Road. Mrs. McPeek gathered logs that had gotten loose from the log booms going down Rainy Lake. Some washed up to shore; others could be found floating nearby. Mr. Anderson prepared the logs for Mrs. McPeek for her to use in building the resort cabins. Once a year, the children from Lake Park School were invited to stay for the week-end. Mrs. McPeek sat in her rocker by her big stone fireplace and read stories to the children. She made treats and taught the children to recite poetry. Her good friend, Ernest Oberholtzer, would also stop by to read stories to the children.

The children would often cross the ice on Jackfish Creek in the winter to visit the Lyon and Weberg families who lived on the other side. Blanche had a close call when she and Florence Larsen fell through the ice on a cold November evening. The girls had been playing in the woods across the creek when they noticed it was getting dark and time for dinner. Helen Larsen and Blanche's younger sister Margaret headed across first, and had reached the other side when they looked back to see Blanche and Florence go through the ice. The girls were thrashing through the water, trying to get to the shore. Helen Larsen showed incredible bravery when she went into the cold water and helped Blanche and Florence to shore. They made it to the Jespersen farm where Huldah wrapped them in blankets, sat them before the fire, and made cocoa to warm them.

The winters were harsh, but somehow the children managed to have fun sledding and having snowball fights during recess. They would often play games, one of the favorites was "Feds and Bootleggers." The children had all heard the stories of the bootleggers and the federal officers. One incident brought it close to home when one of the neighbors, who owned a farm down the road from the school, was arrested for making a very large amount of moonshine. Federal officers could often be seen driving down the county roads of Koochiching County following leads or looking for signs of stills and moonshine.

In the spring, school was always brought outdoors for science class, as the children collected wildflowers and leaves to identify and paste into books. A bird feeder was built outside one of the school house windows, so the students were able to study ornithology first hand. There were spelling bees, recitations of poetry and of historical writings. There were written and oral examinations with report cards home to the parents. Spankings were a rare occurrence. Blanche enjoyed the years she spent at the little school house. She learned a great deal and felt she was ready to move to the new high school in the fall of 1924, when she would start the seventh grade.

The summer before she started high school, Blanche began to work for Mrs. McPeek at Birch Point Resort as a cleaning girl and helper. The resort was located about a mile down the road from the farm at Jackfish Bay. Blanche saved enough money from the job to pay for the new dresses she would wear to the high school in the Falls. She picked the clothes from the catalog with her friend Muriel Johnson. Blanche had a rule that every time she bought a dress for herself, she bought a dress for her mother and her little sister, Margaret. The family had never been wealthy, but they had always had enough, and they were fortunate to have very good friends in the neighbors at Jackfish Bay.

In the summer of 1927, while working for Mrs. McPeek, Blanche had the idea to start making candy to sell at the local resorts. She made peanut brittle, fudge, and divinity. Bob and Lil Williams had recently purchased a resort near Crystal Beach and bought candy to sell there. The candy was delicious and went over so well that Blanche was soon selling it to the resorts all along the lake road. The first summer, she saved enough money to buy an older model T Ford.[56] Blanche was only sixteen years old, and it had taken a lot to talk her dad into letting her buy the automobile. As usual, her mother had convinced him in her quiet way that Blanche could handle the responsibility. She now had transportation to deliver her candy to the businesses all the way to the Falls. Blanche's father even taught her how to keep her own bookkeeping system.

Blanche and Muriel Johnson often spent time at each other's houses during their high school years. Muriel loved staying at the farm with Blanche and her brothers and sister, especially when Blanche's cousins from Loman joined them. The group of girls climbed Blueberry Hill behind the farm where they would pick berries in the summer, sit in the sun and talk, and swim in the lake next to the farmhouse. Muriel was amazed that

---

[56] Wayne Jespersen Interview.

Blanche could swim long distances. Blanche would laugh and say that she could swim all day long.

During their high school years Blanche often visited Muriel in the Falls, where they would often go downtown to the shops and restaurants. Muriel introduced Blanche to Virginia Keyes, the mayor's daughter, and they became great friends. Virginia was a beautiful young woman, she was glamorous and wore a fur coat in the winter. The girls brought Blanche to the hairdresser where she had her long, thick auburn hair bobbed and waved in the new fashion. Blanche was having a wonderful time in high school; her grades were excellent and she genuinely loved school.

Blanche excelled in her studies and graduated from high school in the spring of in 1929. She spent that summer selling her candy and helping on the farm. She was small, energetic, and strong from working hard. Blanche had deep blue eyes and a sprinkle of freckles across her nose. Although she was shy, once she got to know someone she was very funny. Healthy and wholesome, with a lovely complexion, boys were noticing Blanche. She didn't seem to notice them. She still had thoughts of Charlie Williams.

On the first day of school in the fall of 1929, Blanche watched as her younger brothers and sister walked down the road to catch the school bus. She was digging potatoes from the garden for her mother to fix for dinner, and as she dropped the last potato in the basket, she began to cry. Blanche did not cry easily, but this was the worst day of her life because she wasn't getting on the school bus with the others. She had no idea of what she wanted to do with her life, and she would have given anything to be able to go to college, but that was not possible as the family could not afford it. Never one for self-pity, she decided she would keep busy, save her money for the future, and spend time with her friends.[57]

One day at the end of October, Blanche and Helen Larsen met Muriel and some other friends for a picnic in Ranier. The area was experiencing a warm fall and the girls were in high spirits. The girls stopped at Erickson's Grocery and bought lemonade, then walked down Spruce Street to the Ranier School. They set out their picnic, and after they had eaten, sat talking at the top of the school steps.

Muriel told Blanche, "Oh my goodness! I forgot to tell you! Charlie Williams is back in town! I saw him driving his dad's motor car in the Falls yesterday." Blanche looked up and just then, she saw Bob Williams' black Packard pass by the

---

[57] Blanche Williams Oral History.

school, with Charlie driving. John Bishop was in the passenger seat. Her heart jumped when she saw Charlie look at her. Blanche hadn't seen him in two years and they had both changed. She didn't expect Charlie to remember her, but she hoped he did.

PART FOUR: 1929 to 1931

Blueberry Hill

I found my thrill on Blueberry Hill, on Blueberry Hill,

when I found you. Louis Armstrong.

Charlie had many interesting experiences while he was "on the road." He was lucky to have encountered Johnny Johnson on the day he ran away from Ranier, because Johnny helped Charlie survive during the year he spent riding the rails. He and Johnny Johnson worked here and there and saw the country. They stayed in hobo jungles and rode "over the hill" several times, the "hill" being the Sierra Madres Mountains of California.

They met a man in a hobo jungle in Wyoming who was said to be the King of the Hoboes, and listened to his stories around the campfire near the tracks. They outran railway bulls, ate around many hobo campfires, and watched scenery across much of the United States. Charlie had enjoyed himself immensely, but in the fall of 1928 after over a year on the road, he thought it was time that he settled somewhere and found a job.

Charlie heard that there was work to be had in the shipyards of Bremerton, Washington. He and Johnny parted ways since Johnny wasn't ready to settle down. The two boys had seen each other through more than a few scrapes. Both boys were a little choked up when Johnny hugged Charlie goodbye and jumped a side car Pullman headed east out of Bremerton.

Charlie found a job working on the construction of the U.S.S. Louisville and a room in a boarding house nearby. He learned to weld in the shipyard and a lot about motors and machines. He had kept his promise to write to his dad, and the two had made up long before.

The time spent on the road had been good for Charlie. He seemed to lose the anger he felt after his mother's death. Johnny had been worse off than Charlie by a long shot. He lost both of his parents when he was twelve and had been on the road ever since. Charlie had grown up and at twenty years old, he began to miss home and his dad and Lil. He also found himself missing Ranier, Kettle Falls, and Rainy Lake. By the fall of 1929, Charlie decided that it was time to go home. He had saved some money during his time in Bremerton, and he could have easily afforded a railway ticket, but the lure of the jump got the best of him. He hopped an eastbound freight outside of Bremerton and headed toward Minnesota and home.

Please Write or Wire

R. S. WILLIAMS
RANIER - - - MINNESOTA

A memorable event is the boat ride from Ranier, Ash River or Kabetogama to Kettle Falls. Don't forget your camera for your opportunities for truly fine pictures are countless.

Kettle Falls
Hotel

LOCATED on the KETTLE RIVER
At the East End of Renowned

RAINY LAKE
IN MINNESOTA

A TRUE WILDERNESS SETTING
FIFTY MILES BY WATER FROM

RANIER, MINNESOTA
ON THE CANADIAN BORDER

KETTLE FALLS RESORT

Wilderness and Land of the Chippewa 100 Years Ago

IT is still wilderness but the land of the fisherman. Originally filled with moose, deer, bear and beaver this gorgeous virgin forest country first attracted the trappers who pushed westward from the famous Pidgeon River Hudson Bay Post over the great inland waterway of the border lakes—Gunflint, Sagaunga, LaCroix, Namakan and Rainy. This became the Dawson Trail and furs purchased at the Hudson Bay Post at Fort Frances on the west end of Rainy Lake were transported through these lakes and over the portages to the eastern markets. And always, as now, there was a portage at beautiful Kettle Falls where the Kettle River flows out of Namakan Lake into Rainy Lake. For years the fur trade flourished as the fur bearing animals were trapped without restriction. Then came the gold rush of 1898 to Rainy Lake City on Rainy Lake where gold was mined in sufficient quantities to establish a stamping mill. The trail through the waterways became a highway for boat traffic and railway tracks were put in at Kettle Falls to facilitate the portaging of larger boats around the twenty-foot natural drop in the Kettle River where the falling waters over the years had worn the rock in the shape of a huge kettle.

The gold mining operations were short-lived but the picks and shovels of the booted miners were soon replaced by the cant hooks and peavies of the calk-shoed lumberjacks—as hard working and hard drinking crew as ever traversed this great water highway. The logging operations have been carried on for years and great log rafts carrying millions of feet of lumber often filled these lakes from one rocky shore to another—and piling up on the countless islands dotting both Namakan and Rainy Lakes. One big log drive from far away Quetico country was enroute in the water for five years.

To provide a stopping place for the loggers and a haven for hay fever sufferers, the Kettle Falls Resort was built in 1913. Gone are the fur traders, the miners and most of the logging crews but the waters remain—waters teeming with game fish—walleyed pike and great northern pike up to twenty pounds—crappies, bass and perch.

Accommodations
Your Comfort Our First Consideration

HERE, on a veritable island amidst lakes and waterfalls, is an astonishing hotel with a kitchen that cannot be beat in the Borderland. It is Kettle Falls hotel, operated by Mr. and Mrs. "Bob" Williams of Ranier. Built originally to house lumbering officials and woodsmen on their travels between International Falls, Fort Frances and the vast woods which lie to the east, Mr. and Mrs. Williams have transformed it into a tourist hotel of 20 clean comfortable rooms.

Kettle Falls hotel, set back but a short distance, yet within sound of the falls, furnishes first class accommodations for the tourist or fisherman, or for the vacationist who wishes to enjoy peacefully and quietly the beauties of this wonderful region. It is an ideal retreat for hay-fever sufferers, for that malady is non-existent in the clear, healthful atmosphere which is characteristic of this northern wilderness.

Kettle Falls is found at the extreme eastern end of Rainy Lake, in the short stretch of river joining Namakan and Rainy Lakes. Here nature has played a queer trick on mapmakers for at Kettle Falls and only at Kettle Falls can an individual stand on Minnesota soil and look south into Canada.

Board and Room. $7.00 per day

★

• Bar in Connection

188

Charlie was almost home. As he passed through the little towns of Ray and Ericsburg, his anticipation grew. The next stop was Ranier, Minnesota. Seventeen miles later, when the train slowed to a crawl, Charlie jumped from the open boxcar to find himself on the outskirts of Ranier. He was on the east side of the tracks and began to walk north toward the train station.

He could see off to his left that the shanty town was still there and it brought to mind the days at Kettle Falls following his mother's death, when the ladies had been kind to him. It reminded him of the loneliness he had endured, which always brought a kind of sadness. Shaking it off, he thought of Bob and Lil, and his excitement grew at the thought of seeing them again. He hoped that Buster would remember him. There was a chill in the air, and Charlie could see his breath as he walked along side of the slow moving train until he reached the Ranier station. It was the end of October in 1929.

189

When Charlie came close to the center of town, he saw a crowd gathered on the corner of Duluth and Spruce Streets, in front of the bank building. As he came nearer he spotted his dad with a group of his cronies. Bob saw him and broke from them and greeted Charlie with a hug. "What is going on?" Charlie asked. Bob explained that there had been a run on the bank after the stock market crash. People had been screaming at Mr. Anderson, one of the bank owners, demanding to get their money out. Bob said that a lot of people had lost money in the stock market and that bad times were coming. He explained to Charlie that banks were folding across the country, "The bank survived the run today, but Anderson might not be able to hold out on another one." Bob seemed to downplay any losses he may have suffered, but Charlie could see that he was worried.

"Let's go home, Son, and see Lil. She closed up Kettle Falls last month and is home for the winter. She is doing a great job up there, son. Times are changing, and Lil is starting to push the place as a fishing resort! We're getting customers from as far as Chicago to go fishing, if you can believe that. Enough about us, let's get you some food and get you settled. We want to hear all about your adventures."

When they got back to the farmhouse, they found Lil at the kitchen table having coffee with Carrie, who was still working for them. The women were very happy to see Charlie and very relieved that he had made it home safely. When Buster saw Charlie, he jumped on his lap and snuggled there while Charlie related to Bob and Lil some of his adventures on the road, including his friendship with Johnny Johnson, and their scrapes with the railroad bulls.

That evening at dinner, Charlie asked if he could go to work for them in the liquor business. "Dad, I need to make money and it looks like work might be scarce around here, since the crash. I've grown up and I've learned to control my temper. I will be smart, and I promise I won't attract attention to myself. " Bob and Lil finally relented, mainly because the authorities had grown lax since the politicians were talking of repeal.

Bob also hired Charlie to drive to Hurley, Wisconsin, to pick up the acts on the entertainment circuit and bring them back to Ranier. When the performers were done entertaining in Ranier, Charlie would drive them to Ten Strike, Minnesota, a wild town about seventy miles south of the Falls. Charlie would drive the Packard. Bob did say that if Charlie wanted to do a little bootlegging on the side, he wouldn't stop him.

More and more people were agreeing that prohibition had been a failed experiment and they no longer stood for the strong arm tactics some of the officers had used. Three of the federal officers stationed in the Falls had been forced to leave after a petition was filed by a sizable contingent of the population. Bob could feel things changing and he longed for the end of prohibition. He considered himself lucky to have made it through the years without being killed or sent to prison. He had been arrested a few times, but never indicted or convicted. He now only wanted him and his men to come out of it alive, and with his businesses and money intact. He was anxious for the day when he could go legitimate in all of his business dealings.

Bob and Lil told Charlie that they planned to liquidate some of their assets and were considering moving south to Florida to buy a business to operate during the winter months. Bob had already sold some of his land along the beach road, mainly to Frank Keyes and Dan McCarthy, but he would keep the farmhouse until he and Lil were ready to make the move south. Eventually, they planned to spend the summers at Kettle Falls and the winters in Florida. When they eventually sold the hotel in Ranier and the farmhouse, they would rent a room in Ranier from their friend Ossie Lessard during break up and freeze up of the big lake.

The landscape of Ranier was changing since the crash of 1929 and two incidents in the spring of 1930 altered Ranier forever. The Ranier State Bank owners had fought valiantly to hold off the closing of the bank, but the bank finally failed in April of 1930. Some residents lost money with the closing, although most people had withdrawn their money by then.

Added to that, Helma Beaton's Ranier European Hotel was the scene of a terrible fire and burned to the ground shortly after the bank closing. Helma had been operating the hotel on her own since her husband's death many years before, with the help of her brother-in-law Jazzbo Beaton. Bob and George Bailey, along with a few other Ranier residents heard the cries of fire. After seeing the hotel ablaze, they ran to the fire house, which was located near to William's Hotel. The residents battled the fire for hours, but they were unable to save the building. Luckily all the residents of the hotel were able to escape and no one was seriously injured. With the loss of the hotel, Helma went to live with her daughter Hazel, who was married to Charles Houska, a young man who had recently moved to Ranier to work for Jess Rose as a customs agent.

With the closing of the bank, the depression seemed to truly hit the little city. Bob, being one of the more affluent citizens, gave more and more to the poor as the depression deepened. His kitchen at William's Hotel fed more and more people who were unable to afford the price of a meal.

Charlie soon reunited with his friends, John Bishop, Sylvester Keyes, the Couture brothers, and Jack Green, who shared Charlie's love of Rainy Lake and had often been his canoeing partner. Sylvester tried to talk Charlie out of running liquor and said that he could go to work for Sylvester's father at their logging operation. Charlie declined the offer, and instead, he and John Bishop began hauling cases of booze for Bob to the various blind pigs and soft drink parlors around the county. Charlie drove Bob's new black Packard. It was a beautiful vehicle and could outrun anything the police might be driving. Bob came through with his offer, and the boys also drove back and forth between Hurley and Ranier, hauling the band members, singers, and dancers on the entertainment circuit.

Not long after Charlie's return, he and John Bishop were told by Bob's men to drop off six barrels of whiskey in an open boxcar on the east side of the tracks in Ranier, a few blocks past the station. The boxcar's destination was Chicago. The boys were told that they should load the barrels into the boxcar as quickly and quietly as possible, close the door, and leave the area. Charlie and John loaded the whiskey as they were told, closed the door, and left. When they were driving away, Charlie asked, "Where is Buster?" The two boys started to panic when Buster wasn't in the motor car. They parked the car and quietly snuck back through the woods just in time to see Jess Rose and Charles Houska opening the boxcar. Officer Rose had heard Buster barking and walked straight to the whiskey. When Jess reached for Buster, Buster twisted out of his arms, jumped down and ran to the woods, where Charlie grabbed him and made a run for the car. It was so dark that Jess Rose could not see them, but he would swear that he had seen that dog before. Bob's men got a laugh out of the incident, but none of them told Bob because they knew he would fail to see the humor.

A few days later, Charlie and John Bishop dropped off a case of whiskey and gin in Ray, Minnesota, a small village about twenty miles south of the Falls. It was a beautiful fall day and they were in high spirits when they drove back to Ranier. As they passed by the Ranier school house on the edge of town, Charlie saw a girl sitting on the railing of the school steps and asked John, "Who is the dish sitting on the railing?" John replied, "That's Blanche Jespersen from Jespersen's dairy farm. Don't get any ideas about her; she is way out of your league. Her father wouldn't let you near her."

Charlie remembered Blanche Jespersen as the little girl who rode the bus with him years earlier. At that time she had been a skinny kid with long auburn pigtails. It was obvious that she had grown up. Her hair had been long and straight then, but now it was short and waved. She was still small, but she had grown into a very pretty young woman. Charlie was smitten. He tried to think of a way to meet her, but John told him that Blanche had graduated from high school that year, and spent most of her time helping her parents on the farm.

John said that two of Blanche's best friends, Muriel Johnson and Virginia Keyes, were from the Falls and that sometimes Blanche spent time at their houses. Charlie hoped that he might run into her with Sylvester, who was Virginia's cousin, but visits to the Keyes home over the next few weeks proved fruitless.

Early the next spring, Charlie was driving the Packard on the lake road by Jackfish Bay, after dropping off an order at one of the lake resorts with John Bishop. The road was under construction and being extended east towards Tilson Creek; it was very muddy and Charlie soon got the Packard stuck. He told John that he would walk to Jespersen's farm and ask to use the horses to pull the automobile out of the mud. Andy Jespersen answered the door of the farmhouse and agreed to bring the horses out to the road. Charlie caught a glimpse of Blanche in the kitchen and could see that the family was about to have dinner. He could see that her eyes were as blue as Rainy Lake and he could make out the sprinkle of freckles across her nose. When she looked up at him and shyly smiled, he felt a physical jolt.

Andy Jespersen brought the horses down to the road and the Packard was soon free and the boys were on their way. "Did you do that on purpose to see Blanche?" John asked. "Of course not, but she sure is sweet." Charlie answered.

Blanche Jespersen 1930

The Ranier School had a large hall that the residents were able to use for basket socials several times each year and Blanche and her friends usually attended. Charlie and John Bishop, with John's girlfriend, went to the spring social at the Ranier school at Charlie's insistence. Charlie was hoping that he might see Blanche Jespersen there. He wasn't disappointed; she was standing with a group of girls at the edge of the hall. Charlie waited a few minutes until she took a seat and then he approached her.

They made small talk for a few minutes, and then Charlie asked, "Have you ever been to Canada, Blanche?" Blanche looked up at him and answered, "Of course I have, why?" "My friends and I are going for a ride to the Emperor Hotel and we wondered if you would like to join us." Blanche had never been to the Emperor Hotel, but she had heard that the hotel was beautiful and that the food was excellent. "If I go with you, I have to be home by 10 o'clock. Do you promise that you will bring me home by then?" "You have my word, Blanche." He said. Blanche told him to meet her outside and that she would tell her friends she was leaving. The Emperor was located in downtown Fort Frances, right across the Rainy River from the

Falls. The two towns were connected by a narrow bridge that Backus had built in 1912.

Blanche could not believe that she was riding in a Packard with Charlie Williams and going to a restaurant in Canada that served beer! She didn't think Charlie would ever notice her, and yet he had sought her out. She had hoped that she might see him after he had come to the farm. Here she was drinking beer and eating pretzels! Blanche didn't think much of the beer, but she loved the pretzels.[58]

The two couples had a great time laughing and talking that night. Charlie introduced Blanche to his love of jazz, as the Emperor had a great band playing. They danced to the music of Louis Armstrong and Duke Ellington. As ten o'clock approached, they had one final dance to Charlie's favorite song, *The St. Louis Blues*. They left soon after to be sure that Blanche was home on time. She thought that he might try to kiss her when he said goodnight at the end of the farm drive, but he didn't. He did tell her that he wanted to see her again.

---

[58] Blanche Williams Oral History

The next morning, Blanche woke to hear her mother on the party line telephone with one of the neighbors. "That's not possible. Blanche was at a social at the school in Ranier last night." Huldah Jespersen said. "I will ask her about it right now, but I am sure you are wrong."

Blanche pretended to be sleeping when her mother entered the bedroom. "Blanche dear, Mrs. Lindstrom just told me the craziest story about you riding in a car with Bob Williams's boy last night!" "Mother, please don't tell Dad. I went for a ride with Charlie because I really like him. He was a perfect gentleman and we weren't alone." Blanche pleaded. Her mother answered, "I'm sure he is a nice boy, Blanche, but your father is bound to hear about this. Nothing stays a secret around here, and you know that. I'm sure that everyone on the party line was listening just now."

For the next few days, Blanche waited for her father to mention her ride with Charlie. When he hadn't said anything for a week, she realized that her mother hadn't told him. She felt guilty for putting her mother in that position, but found it terribly unfair that Charlie would be judged because of what his father did. She had had a crush on Charlie Williams for as long as she could remember, and she wanted to see him again.

Blanche didn't see Charlie until a couple of months later, when she was selling her homemade candy at the resorts in the area. Bob Williams still owned a resort on Crystal Beach where Blanche had been selling candy for the past two few summers. Charlie was sitting on the porch of the resort with his little dog when he saw Blanche drive up and screech to a halt in her Model T Ford. Charlie chuckled to himself when he saw her. He couldn't believe his luck! Despite his efforts, he hadn't seen Blanche since the night at the Emperor. After they talked for a few minutes, Charlie asked if he could take her to dinner at the resort and she accepted. Blanche, being an animal lover, petted and fussed over Buster, which he loved.

Later that evening, they took a walk across Jespersen's field and climbed Blueberry Hill. There, sitting side by side watching the sunset, Charlie kissed Blanche for the first time. They were both shaken, and Charlie said, "I think we will have to get married, Blanche." She laughed and said that she had been thinking the same thing. Holding hands, the two walked back through the field and kissed goodbye at the car. As Blanche turned to cross the road to the farm driveway, she saw a sheriff's car drive off in the distance, heading towards town. She hoped they hadn't been seen. More important, she hoped it hadn't been her Uncle Vic Linsten driving, who was the deputy sheriff from Loman, for he would surely tell her parents.

From then on, Charlie and Blanche found every opportunity to see each other. When someone finally mentioned seeing them together, Andy Jespersen was furious. He refused to say who had seen them, but he told Blanche she was not allowed to keep company with a bootlegger's son. Blanche pleaded with Andy and told him that she really liked Charlie and that he hadn't done anything wrong. Andy told Blanche that he was worried about her keeping company with Charlie because Bob Williams associated with some very dangerous people. Blanche scoffed at the idea and said that Charlie was a gentleman and that he would never let anyone hurt her. Andy could not be persuaded to change his mind and from then on it was even more difficult for the young people to see each other. Blanche's father kept a close eye on her, and she wasn't able to see Charlie until a chance encounter gave them the opportunity.

During the first two decades of the twentieth century, several wealthy industrialists from Minneapolis and other cities discovered Rainy Lake and constructed grand summer homes there.

203

Many were friends of Ernest Oberholtzer and several of them had originally come from his home town of Davenport, Iowa. They often came to Jespersen's farm by boat to buy milk and to use the telephone, as it was the last stop on the lake telephone line. Some of them parked their automobiles at the farm and waited there to be picked up by the launches belonging to the lake lodges, as Jespersen's farm was also the last stop on the road system. Blanche's mother, Huldah Jespersen, was a favorite of Mrs. Ford Bell and some of the other society ladies. The women often visited with Mrs. Jespersen in the Jespersen living room while waiting to be picked up by the launches.[59]

One day in the spring of 1931, Ernest Oberholtzer came to Jespersen's farm to buy milk, as he regularly did. Mr. Oberholtzer lived on Mallard Island, which was located a few miles up Rainy Lake from the farm on Jackfish Bay. He had built several cabins on the island and often had his friends from New York City and other glamorous places to visit. He also frequently entertained the wealthy lodge owners.

Mr. Oberholtzer had recently lost his mother, who had acted as his housekeeper at the island. Blanche had known Mr. Oberholtzer since she was a little girl going to Lake Park School

---

[59] Conversation with Mrs. Ford Bell

when he would read stories to the children. He was often at Mrs. McPeek's and had seen Blanche working there for the last few summers. When Mr. Oberholtzer saw Blanche helping her mother in the kitchen that day, he offered her a summer job working at Mallard Island as a cleaning girl and cook's helper.[60] Blanche took the job gladly, mostly to get away from the situation at home regarding her and Charlie's friendship.

Mallard Island was a retreat for poets, musicians, writers, and Mr. Oberholtzer's conservationist friends. They had won a hard fight against E.W. Backus over the building of a string of sixteen dams along the chain of border lakes. Because of the efforts of Mr. Oberholtzer and his friends, most of the boundary waters would remain intact for the generations. In addition to the dam at the Falls, Backus built a dam at Kenora, a dam at Lake of the Woods, and two dams at Kettle Falls, one on each side of the border.

Backus had been stopped from further construction by the Quetico-Superior Council and the Wilderness Society; Mr. Oberholtzer was a founding member of both organizations. The additional dams would have controlled the water system for a hundred miles along the border between the United States and

---

[60] Blanche Williams Oral History

Canada, all the way to Ely, Minnesota, and would have changed drastically some of the most pristine wilderness in the United States. Mallard Island served as the real headquarters for both organizations.[61]

Blanche was fond of Mr. Oberholtzer. She had a great deal of respect for him and loved working on Mallard Island. She had her own room in the cook's cabin, which sat in a quiet, secluded cove on the island. Ober, as his friends called him, was a kind man. Well educated and intelligent, he had many books and musical instruments on the island. Blanche was an avid reader and soaked up the culture there. Mr. Oberholtzer had studied landscape architecture. Beautiful rock gardens decorated the island and sat in various places near the cabins that he had built. The cabins were all given names, such as the Artist's House, the Bird House, the Cedar Bark house, the Front House, the Japanese House, the Library, the Wannigan, Ober's Summer House, and the Winter House.[62]

---

[61] Minnesota Historical Society Oberholtzer Papers
[62] Ernest Oberholtzer Foundation website

One day when Blanche was done with her work, she asked Mr. Oberhotzer if there was anything else she could do to keep busy. "Does anything need painting?" She asked. "I love to paint." Ober said that she could paint anything she wanted to paint, so Blanche spent a good part of that summer painting furniture and accents in the cabins in a variety of beautiful Scandinavian colors.[63]

One evening in early June, when Blanche had just finished her work in the Wannigan,[64] she heard a boat pull up to the dock in the bay. This was no surprise as many people came to visit Ober, but when Blanche looked out the window and saw that it was Charlie, her heart skipped a beat. She ran down to the dock and stood and waited while he tied up the boat. They sat and talked for a while and then Charlie asked if she would like to go for a boat ride. Charlie had just purchased the sixteen foot wood Larson boat and was excited that he had been able to buy a new outboard motor from his friend George Finstad in Ranier. George was known as a mechanical genius and had patents on

---

[63] Oral history of June Williams Dougherty
[64] Floating kitchen

parts of the Johnson Evinrude outboard motor. Charlie spent a lot of time visiting with George at his boat works and learned a great deal about outboard motors from him.

The boat provided Charlie with his own transportation around the lake and it gave him a great sense of freedom. He took meticulous care of the boat, and he was excited to show Blanche, and to take her for a boat ride. It was a beautiful evening with a gorgeous sunset; the deep blue water was like glass.

Charlie drove slowly out of the bay. He stopped the boat and they drifted in the middle of the lake. "I know I joked about this, Blanche, but I really was serious. I've been crazy about you since the first time I saw you. I've been thinking that I want to ask your father for his permission for us to see each other. I know he isn't crazy about me, but I am going to find a straight job. I will work really hard, Blanche, I promise. I might even go back to school at Dunwoody in Minneapolis to learn more about motors. No more bootlegging for me. I told my dad and he is happy because he didn't want me to run liquor anyway." She replied, "Charlie, I would love nothing more, but I don't think my father would approve. My mother knows how we feel about each other, and maybe she will help me. Let's see what happens when I go home in September."

All that summer, Charlie came to visit Blanche on her days off. They fished or picked berries; Charlie cooked delicious shore lunches of walleyed pike, fried potatoes, and bacon sandwiches.

They both loved to swim and stopped at any number of beautiful beaches to take a dip in the lake. Blanche could swim long distances. Charlie would often slowly drive the boat next to her while she made a long distance swim. Charlie always brought his little dog Buster and he enjoyed riding in the bow of the boat, with his little face to the wind. When he grew tired, he would climb under the bow and take a nap.

Blanche had never been to Kettle Falls and Charlie wanted her to see where he had spent so much of his time while growing up. Kettle Falls was about forty miles up Rainy Lake from Jespersen's farm and Blanche's father had never had more than a rowboat or a canoe at the farm.

They planned the trip on a hot day in early August, on Blanche's day off. Charlie arrived at Mallard Island early that morning. Blanche had packed a lunch for them and was waiting at the dock when Charlie pulled up in his new boat. Charlie drove the new motor from the back of the boat, as the motor had a tiller handle. Blanche sat on the opposite side, one seat up from him, facing the front.

They headed due east for several miles until they reached an opening along the shore that led to Brule Narrows. They entered the narrows and Charlie skillfully maneuvered through the channel. The lake was like glass when they came out on the other side onto big Rainy.

Blanche had never seen anything so beautiful as the east end of Rainy Lake. Granite cliffs, huge pine trees, and beautiful beaches dotted the shore line. Charlie told her that he always felt like he was coming home when he drove out of the Brule. As they proceeded east, she noticed that there were several logging camps and a lot of the big pine trees had been cutover on the peninsula. Charlie told her that a lot of the loggers spent their time off at Kettle Falls. He pointed out the opening to Kempton Channel, an alternate route if the wind came up.

They headed east across the big lake for another hour until they reached the American Channel, a short winding river that led to Kettle Falls and the hotel that Charlie's father and mother owned. Blanche was surprised by all of the activity going on when they reached the Kettle Falls dock below the American dam. There were many people milling around several shacks that lined the shore. Charlie explained that most of them were called blind pigs and that people drank liquor there.

Charlie said he was surprised to see men at the dock with fishing gear and stringers of fish. Everyone seemed to know Charlie. Several ladies called out to him as they docked the boat and headed up the boardwalk to the hotel. Blanche started to ask him who the ladies were when he began to tell her about them. "Some people think that these ladies are bad," he said, "but nothing could be further from the truth. They have just had a bad shake. After my mother died, I was really alone. I was so sad, Blanche, I thought I might die, too. I don't know what I would have done without the ladies before my dad married Lil. They were very kind to me. I know that they are looked down upon by some of the people of Ranier." She squeezed his hand and said, "I am sure they are kind ladies, Charlie."

When they were halfway up the walk, Blanche could hear the nickelodeon playing from the bar. They walked up the steps and entered the porch to see several of men sitting in the wicker chairs, a few with girls on their laps; they all yelled hello to Charlie.

Charlie brought Blanche into the lobby, where men sat around several tables, playing cards. A man was playing the piano and people were singing along. They walked through the dining room to get to the kitchen, where they found Lil cooking behind a huge wood stove. Several men sat around the large kitchen table drinking coffee and visiting with her. Lil came to greet them, and greeted Charlie with a hug. "Mom, this is my girlfriend, Blanche Jespersen. Blanche, this is my mother, Lil Williams."

With her hand on her hip, Lil looked Blanche over and said, "You must be the dairy farmer's daughter who sells candy at the resorts. I've made some candy in my day, even had a candy store before I married Charlie's dad. Come on in, and don't pay any mind to the characters around this place. Most of them are harmless." Lil told Charlie to get them each a cup of egg coffee, which was already made in a big camp coffee pot on the stove.

Just then, a very old man with ragged clothes, hair to his shoulders, and bare feet walked in to the kitchen. He carried a tall walking stick and looked like he hadn't had a bath in a long time. Blanche wasn't sure how to react, when Charlie saved her by saying, "Blanche, this is Catamaran. He lives in a cave at Squirrel Narrows about a mile from here. He has the most beautiful garden you ever saw."

Lil introduced Blanche to Carrie Shehan and Josie Kervan, who both had worked for Bob and Lil for years. The women both had a hug for Charlie and warmly welcomed

212

Blanche. Charlie and Blanche sat and visited with Lil, Carrie, and Josie for a while. They stopped at the porch on the on the way out of the hotel, where Charlie introduced Blanche to his friend, Oscar Nelson. Oscar lived in a log cabin nearby and trapped in the winter. Blanche liked him immediately. He had come from Sweden like her Grandmother Anna Hoard's family, and he reminded her of the old trappers that lived in Loman where Blanche had been born.

As they were leaving, Blanche asked Charlie if they were going to see the bar room. Charlie laughed and said that they would save that for another day.

Charlie and Blanche spent the rest of the afternoon exploring the trails around Kettle Falls. Late that afternoon they said goodbye to Lil, and then set off in the boat to head down Rainy Lake. After leaving the American Channel, Charlie veered left off of the big lake and headed along the south shore through a series of beautiful islands. They continued for a few miles until they reached the opening for Kempton Channel.

Charlie stopped the boat there, took her hands in his and said, "This spot is near to the lumber camp I want to work at this winter. I am hoping they might have a cook's helper job for you, too. I want you to marry me, Blanche. I love you so much. I will work hard and make you proud of me, and I promise I will

213

never leave you." Blanche nodded yes, trying not to cry. "I hope my father gives his blessing, but either way, the answer is yes."

The sun was just setting when they arrived back at Mallard Island. It had been quite an experience for Blanche and she decided that she liked Kettle Falls very much and that she was going to love being Mrs. Charlie Williams. There was never a dull moment when Charlie was around.

For the rest of the summer, Charlie and Blanche spent as much time together as they could, and planned a life together. Charlie was done with bootlegging and he had talked to Henry Keyes about him and Blanche working at one of his logging camps during the winter after they were married. He would have applied for a job in the paper mill in the Falls, but the mill had been forced to close because Mr. Backus had gone bankrupt. Charlie was very lucky to have Sylvester Keyes as a friend because chances were good that his father was going to hire him, and jobs were scarce since the crash.

In September when Blanche was home on the farm, she and Charlie met on Blueberry Hill whenever they could get away. Charlie planned to speak to Blanche's father about them getting married, but he was waiting for formal word about the job from Henry Keyes. Ercil, Blanche's cousin from Loman, often visited the farm and she helped Charlie and Blanche by passing messages between the two.

Ercil often accompanied Charlie and Blanche when they went dancing and listening to jazz at the *Emperor* and the other hotspots in Fort Frances, where they weren't as likely to be seen. For the first time, Charlie brought Blanche to visit Bob and Lil at the farmhouse by the beach. Lil was back from her summer at Kettle Falls, where she was still pushing the place as a fishing resort. Bob and Lil were planning a trip to Florida after the first of the year, and were talking about buying a business in Key Largo. Blanche knew Bob and Lil from selling her candy and they had always been generous and pleasant to her.

Bob and Lil had recently received the terrible news that Bob's good friend, Cap Thompson, had died unexpectedly. Cap Thompson was one of Bob's best friends and had piloted the *Mayflower* since Bob purchased the boat. He was considered to be one of the best pilots on Rainy Lake and had become a legend by outrunning and outfoxing the federal agents for years. Bob

215

and Lil were both shocked and saddened by the captain's death. Bob was going through a hard time and Lil was worried about him when he didn't seem to be getting past it. Bob was tired, tired of eluding the police, and tired of breaking the law.

On top of Cap's death, that year on Valentine's Day, most of George Moran's gang had been executed by Capone's gang in a Chicago north side garage. The gang had masqueraded as police officers. Moran had narrowly survived, because he was running late that morning, and had seen the men in uniform as he was about to cross the street to enter the garage. After the massacre, Moran began to extricate himself from the liquor business, as he wanted to survive prohibition.

Bob was looking forward to the repeal when he might be able to live a normal life again. He thought about how much prohibition must have cost the country in lives and in money. The cost was unimaginable. The money he alone had seen pass hands he never would have dreamed of. He and Lil were looking forward to another trip to Europe next summer. Charlie and Blanche could stay at the farm while they were gone. He wouldn't worry so much about Charlie now that he had found Blanche.

On a cold day in the beginning of November in 1931, Charlie drove to Jespersen's farm to see Blanche's father. Charlie had been hired by Keyes logging company and felt fortunate to have gotten the job. He saw Andy Jespersen and had a conversation with him, but he didn't tell Blanche what was said, just that he had tried to do the right thing. After talking things over, the couple decided they would be married before Charlie went to work at the logging camp in Kempton Channel, which was located thirty miles up Rainy Lake on the way to Kettle Falls. He would be leaving as soon as the logging season was under way in December.

Mr. Keyes agreed to give Blanche a job as a cookee at the camp,[65] and told Charlie that the couple could have their own cabin there. They would make a good salary to save money to buy or build a house of their own. Blanche and Charlie both told their parents they planned to be married. Huldah could see that Blanche was in love and she wanted the best for her. She couldn't help but like Charlie, he seemed so sincere about his intentions and obviously he was in love with Blanche. Andy

---

[65] Cook's helper at logging camp.

thought Blanche was too young to get married; he was still upset that Blanche had kept the relationship a secret, but he knew he could not stop her. She was nineteen years old and could do as she pleased. Blanche only hoped that her father would learn to accept Charlie. Andy was a good man, but he could be stubborn at times.

On December 3, 1931, Blanche and her cousin Ercil put on their best suits. Blanche packed her bags and put them in the Model T. Blanche drove them to the Williams farmhouse on the lake road, where Charlie was waiting in the Packard with Sylvester Keyes. Ercil would be Blanche's maid of honor and Sylvester would be Charlie's best man.

Charlie and Blanche were married that day at the Koochiching County Courthouse by Judge Wright. Charlie would have seen the irony if he had remembered that this was the judge who had overseen his adoption proceeding in this very courtroom.

There was a small party for the couple afterwards at Bob and Lil's farmhouse.[66] Charlie presented Blanche with a beautiful crystal necklace and earrings as a wedding gift. Murial played the piano and everyone danced and sang along. The big bear

---

[66] Marriage License Charlie Williams and Blanche Jespersen.

218

rugs that lay on the polished wood floors of the living room and dining room were pushed aside for the dancers. The Couture boys, Sylvester Keyes, John Bishop, Jack Green, Virginia Keyes, Helen Larsen and other friends joined them. Lil was glad to see that Bob looked very happy as he watched the newlyweds.

Andy Jespersen may have been against the marriage, but Bob Williams was thrilled with the match. He loved Blanche from the start and had been impressed with her hard work and her natural business abilities when she sold her candy at his resort at Crystal Beach. He would always remember that she drove her own model T Ford that she bought with her own money when she was only sixteen years old. He considered Blanche to be an extremely talented and intelligent young woman, and had no doubt that she would be a wonderful wife and partner to Charlie.

Bob was very happy that his son had found the love of his life, and he had high hopes that Charlie would be lucky in love. He was also confident that Andy Jespersen would eventually accept Charlie, once he got to know him. It was obvious that the kid was head over heels in love with his daughter. Andy would see how hard Charlie was willing to work to be a good provider.

Charlie rented an apartment in the bank building in Ranier on the corner of Spruce and Duluth Streets, the same corner where Bob had first seen Cora so many years before. The couple planned to spend a few days together at the apartment and then Charlie would report to the logging camp at Kempton Channel. Blanche would stay at the apartment until the lake was safe for travel. As soon as the ice was strong enough to support a horse and sleigh, Charlie would be back for her. They would keep the apartment and return to live there in the spring.

Before Charlie left, he took her in his arms and whispered in her ear, "I will be back for you, Mrs. Williams." Blanche watched him as he headed down Spruce Street toward Sand Bay, where he would put on his snow shoes and head east. Charlie walked the thirty miles up the newly frozen lake to Keyes's logging camp at Kempton Channel. He had his heavy pack on his back, but he didn't think of the weight, or the danger; he was in such high spirits he could have run the distance.

Blanche didn't quite know what to do with herself after Charlie was gone. She walked across the street to her new father-in-law's hotel and found Bob in the hotel dining room having coffee and reading *The Baudette Region.* She sat down at the table and picked up part of the paper, a comfortable silence developed between them. Bob chuckled at the latest and said, "That Billy Noonan is a character."

Blanche shyly asked if he might teach her how to cook some of his specialties. "I learned to bake from my mother and from working at Mr. Oberholtzer's island," she said, "but I'm nervous about cooking for all of the workers at the camp."

Bob was used to cooking for a crowd and he was more than happy to help her. The two spent hours cooking at Bob's restaurant and within a few weeks Blanche felt much more comfortable with the task ahead of her at the logging camp. They would love Bob's homemade pancakes and other treats, and they were bound to relish his fried chicken and walleyed pike. The two cemented their relationship and the cooking lessons helped to pass the time until Charlie came for her.

For the first time, Blanche saw the nightclub acts that Bob hired at William's Hotel in Ranier from the entertainment circuit. Andy Jespersen would not have approved or been impressed, but Blanche thoroughly enjoyed the music and dancing. She even saw the famous "Beef Trust" that consisted of several large women who could really sing, and were very light on their feet despite their bulk.

Gamblers at Williams Hotel circa 1920

Ranier Characters circa 1920

On December 20th, Jess Rose received word from Charles Houska, who was on duty at the Ranier railroad depot, that a load of shingles shipped from Canada in two boxcars weighed in much heavier than would have been expected. The railroad agents were trained to look for such discrepancies in weight, as many times the difference was made up in smuggled whiskey. Jess made his way to the depot and ordered his men to unload the two boxcars, where inside they found seventy-nine barrels of good Canadian whiskey. It was the biggest bust ever been made during Jess's tenure. He had a good idea who the shingles and whiskey belonged to, but since the names on the invoices were unknown to him, from Canada and probably fictitious, no arrest could be made. The barrels of whiskey were hauled to the bank building and stored there until they could be destroyed. The shingles would be auctioned by the government at a later date.

Blanche happened to look out the north window of the apartment to see the commotion going on at the railroad depot. She could see a group of men in uniform unloading barrels from two boxcars. Blanche grabbed her coat and ran down the stairs and across the street to find Bob just exiting the hotel. From the look on his face, she could see that something was wrong, but he gave her a smile and said, "Don't worry, dear, it's only money." As it turned out, it was a lot of money, about $63,000 worth of whiskey on the streets of Chicago.

On Christmas Eve, Charlie drove the thirty miles down a frozen Rainy Lake in the horse and sleigh he had borrowed from Henry Keyes. Blanche saw him approach from the window of the apartment. She ran down the stairs and out the door. Charlie jumped down from the sleigh and took her in his arms. They surprised Bob and Lil at the farmhouse and spent a wonderful evening with them.

They had until New Year's Day to prepare to leave for the logging camp where they would spend the rest of the winter. Charlie would bring supplies for the camp as well.

A few days before the newlyweds were set to leave for the logging camp, the authorities came to the bank building and began removing the confiscated barrels of whiskey that were to be destroyed at the lower city dock. Hearing the commotion downstairs, Charlie and Blanche ran down the stairs and exited the building, heading toward the city dock. It seemed that most of the Ranier residents were there to watch and most of them carried a receptacle of some sort. This was big news as there had never been a bust of this size. Jess Rose stood and watched as Charles Houska and other agents rolled the barrels out onto the ice and began breaking them up with axes.

Several Ranier men ran down to the lake and began to fill their jugs and pails, but Rose yelled out for them to stop. Not giving up entirely, many of them scooped the whiskey up in their hands and drank as much as they could. Blanche and Charlie stood near Jess Rose as he barked out orders to his men. Blanche looked up to see Bob walking toward them. As he came nearer, Bob stopped next to Jess Rose and could be heard to say innocently, "What's all the commotion about?" Rose looked at him with a wry expression and replied, "You know damn well what this is all about." Within a couple of hours, many of the good people of Ranier were under the influence of that fine Canadian whiskey. It was never proven who owned the whiskey and no arrests were ever made, but the owner paid a pretty price for it.

Ranier bust circa 1931 – Whiskey barrels being destroyed on the ice. Courtesy of KCHS

On New Year's Eve, the day before Charlie and Blanche were to set out for Kempton Channel, they stopped by the Jespersen farm to visit Blanche's family. They brought Christmas presents for Blanche's parents and for Harold, Margaret, and Wayne, Blanche's brothers and sister. Blanche had missed her family since her elopement and she hoped that the visit would start to heal the relationship with her father. Huldah was very pleasant, but Andy was still unhappy about the marriage. He did smile and shake Charlie's hand when Charlie offered it. Her mother whispered to Blanche as she walked toward the door, "Don't worry dear, your father is getting used to the idea. He does want you to be happy." Blanche replied, "I hope so, Mother, I miss the family very much." Blanche hugged her mother and walked out the door.

Early on New Year's Day, Charlie and Blanche set off from Ranier across Sand Bay in the horse and sleigh; they would head east for about twenty miles, cross the portage at Lost Bay, and reach the logging camp at Kempton Channel by late afternoon. Charlie had prepared the cabin for them. Blanche was bundled in fur blankets with Buster on her lap and Charlie had the reins. He began to sing "I Found My Thrill on Blueberry

Hill," a popular jazz song of the day, and a reference to their first kiss. Blanche laughed at the memory and because she loved the sound of his strong clear voice. This man would be her husband and partner from then on. She put all of her trust in him that day as she had from the very beginning. As for Charlie, he would always say that his life began the day he met her.

The End

Ranier, Minnesota today - Courtesy of City of Ranier

Kettle Falls circa 1970   Williams postcard

Charlie and Blanche Williams and the Kettle Falls Hotel -1970s

Epilogue

Bob and Lil went through with their plans to winter in south Florida. They sold the farmhouse in the mid-thirties and bought a resort on Key Largo, Florida. After prohibition, things settled down in Ranier. Many of the commercial fishermen and business people who are mentioned in this book stayed in Ranier and raised their families there. Many of their ancestors live in Ranier to this day. Bob and Jess Rose remained friends and were both founding members of the International Falls Elks Club in 1936.

Blanche and Charlie returned to Ranier and their apartment in the Ranier Bank Building after the winter at the logging camp. Andy Jespersen forgave his daughter and welcomed Charlie into the Jespersen family and even into his birthday whist club, where Jess Rose was also a member.

Charlie worked cutting timber for Henry Keyes until he was hired at the paper mill in the Falls in the early thirties. Charlie and Blanche had their first two children, June Karen and Dale Randolph, while living in the apartment in the bank building. Blanche sometimes had to carry water from the river to the bank building to wash clothes, so she was happy when they moved to a small cottage at Crystal Beach, where their third child was born, Robert Harold. The Williams family lived in the cottage at Crystal Beach until the late forties when they moved to a house on 12th Avenue in the Falls, where Michael Wayne, Charles Andrew, and Peggy Ann were born. Charlie worked as a millwright in the paper mill for at least twenty years. He loved his job and made many good friends there. He was active in union and government activities, even serving as alderman for the City of International Falls. Blanche was active in the DOES, and cooked many meals at the Elks Club with her friends Bessie Davis, Sharon Saari, Helen Robinson, Pauline Biondich, Stella Frederickson, and others.

At Lil's request, Charlie and Blanche took over the operation of the Kettle Falls Hotel after Bob's death from heart disease in 1956. Lil spent summers at Kettle Falls with the family until her death in 1961. Mike, Chuck, and Peggy Ann, the youngest children, lived at the hotel every summer and began working during the summers at a young age. Many of the grandchildren worked at the hotel in the summers during their teenage years. June and her husband, Bill Dougherty, came to Kettle Falls every weekend for at least twenty years to help. Their three boys spent all of their summers there as well. Billy was the fishing guide, Charlie was the boat pilot, and Tom was a mechanic and Grandpa Charlie's helper. All the grandchildren either came to help on the weekends or stayed to work for the summer. Blanche's brother, Harold Jespersen, spent time at the hotel while logging for Alfred Johnson near Kettle Falls. Blanche's sister, Margaret Casey and her daughter Sherri helped on the weekends.

Many good times were had and lifelong friendships were formed. A large rectangular table sat in the old kitchen of the Kettle Falls Hotel, and held countless coffee breaks and visits, and Williams' family breakfasts, lunches, and dinners. There was great conversation, much laughter, and a great deal of love at that table through four generations of the Williams family over the course of seventy years.

Charlie and Blanche sold the Kettle Falls Hotel to the National Park Service in the late seventies and retired to Fort Lauderdale, Florida. Mike and Chuck, the two youngest sons, operated the hotel as concessionaires until 1994. Blanche and Charlie traveled extensively and had a great deal of fun with the family and their many friends in their retirement. Their marriage lasted for sixty years and their love only grew stronger with time. Charlie and Blanche died three weeks apart at the ages of eighty-four and eighty in the winter of 1992. They are dancing in heaven.

Author's Note

My father rarely talked about his youth, but when pressed he always said that he had a difficult childhood, that he didn't like to dwell on it, and that he liked to think that his life began the day he met my mother. I knew that he had grown up in Ranier, Minnesota, during the prohibition era, that his mother died when he was twelve years old, and that afterwards he had been sent to live in several foster homes. He said that he was eventually adopted by Bob Williams soon after Bob married Lil King in 1921. Bob and Lil operated Williams Night Club in Ranier until it burned down in the 1940s and the Kettle Falls Hotel until their deaths in 1956 and 1961, respectively.

Dad knew little about his biological father, except for his name, John Dickson Keenan, and the fact that Keenan had abandoned his mother and him in Duluth, Minnesota, in 1908, a few days before he was born. He also told us that his mother Cora was disowned by her family in Superior and that he didn't meet any of them until he was an adult. Dad eventually developed a close relationship with his aunts in Superior. When they visited, it was obvious that Hannah, Hazel, and Serine all adored him. Junie remembers Grandma Bertha sending cookies to the

234

family when she was a child. I think connecting with his mother's family meant a lot to Dad.

Through the years, usually when we were traveling by boat to Kettle Falls, Dad often told stories about the old days in Ranier, about the days of prohibition, the commercial fisherman and boats on Rainy Lake, and about the people and life at Kettle Falls. He didn't often include personal details, but mostly described the characters from Ranier and the hotel. Those funny and sometimes sad stories often contained offhanded phrases about his life. He often told stories about his adoptive father, Bob Williams, and that he was a major bootlegger in northern Minnesota during prohibition.

Once when I was a little girl driving through Ranier with Dad, he began to point out some of the houses he had lived in while he was growing up. I remember wondering why he had lived in so many houses, not realizing until much later that those houses were the foster homes he had run away from. He also pointed to where his father's hotel and nightclub had been, now the site of the Ranier Post Office.

Dad pointed out a residential neighborhood in the southeast corner of Ranier that had been called Shantytown, where the "girls" lived in little houses and shacks, and that the ladies had been nice to him when he was a child, as many of them lived at Kettle Falls during the summers.

Dad said that there had been many saloons and blind pigs in Ranier when he was a boy, and that Ranier had been a wild frontier town when he had come there with his mother in 1911, when he was three years old. He said very little about his mother, saying that he didn't remember her very well, although he said she was tall and pretty. He knew that his mother had been disowned by her family and that she was buried in the Olsen family plot in Eau Claire, Wisconsin, without a headstone. He knew that he had an uncle who had been a war hero, but didn't remember anything else about him.

One summer when I was living on our houseboat in the back bay of my sister June's family business, Rainy Lake Houseboats, I asked Dad if I could interview him about his life. He agreed to come over for coffee in the morning and we would talk. I had my tape recorder ready. When I began to ask him questions, he suddenly changed his mind and said that he couldn't do it. He said that terrible things had happened and that he didn't want to revisit them.

For sixty years, Dad carried the same picture of mother in his wallet. Mother is standing in front of a birch tree at the farm. She is laughing in the picture, and the wind is blowing her hair. I asked her once at one of their great anniversary parties at the Elks Club in the Falls, how they had stayed in love for all of those years. She laughed and said that there had never been a dull moment. Of all the gifts our parents gave us, the most precious was their great love for one another. Mother told many stories about her and Dad, how they met, about their early life together, and about their elopement in December of 1931.

Shortly after Dad's death, my sister June was going through his papers and found an outline that he had written about his life in Ranier and at Kettle Falls in the early days. When I saw the outline, I felt like I had won the lottery. Maybe Dad did want to tell his story after all. I vowed to myself that someday when I was older and less busy raising my family, I would try to fill in the blanks of the outline. For the time being, I filed it away with my family papers.

Several years later I was living in Ranier and working as the Ranier City Clerk/Treasurer. Our family lived just a few blocks from the community building. Ironically, our house was built in a residential neighborhood that was once part of the Ranier shantytown.

Shortly after I started the job, I was cleaning the big safe in my office, as I had begun a project to inventory all of the old records, birth and death certificates, and such. I was excited to find the big old jail keys and billy club in a drawer in the safe, and then I noticed something else.

There in the very back of the drawer, was a very old pearl handled pistol and holster, wrapped in a chamois cloth. I was surprised and intrigued to see that written on the gun holster was the owner's name, R.S. Williams, my grandfather. My mind immediately went to the outline. I went home after work and found it.

Certain facts stated in this book were well known to our family, which was helpful, but there were gaping holes in the story. For the next seven years, my daughter Katie and I spent many hours researching Ranier's past in the city minutes and old records, in the local newspaper archives, the county library, the Koochiching County Museum, the National Park Service, and at the Koochiching County Courthouse, where we pored through volumes of documents in order to fill in the blanks of Dad's outline.

My sister and I asked the court to unseal Dad's adoption records, and Judge Charles LeDuc was kind enough to let us review the records for a day. Those papers revealed details about our biological grandfather, John Dickson Keenan, and the life of our grandmother, Cora Olsen Keenan. The documents also described Bob Williams's attempts to legally adopt Dad. Slowly, a story began to emerge and after all the years, I finally started to write. As it turned out, the little city of Ranier, Minnesota turned out to be amazingly rich in characters and history.

Thank You.

Peggy Ann Vigoren

Acknowledgments

Thank you to Kim Nuthak and the staff at the Ranier Clerk's Office for letting me research the old records that were so crucial to the story. Thanks to Mayor Wagner and the Ranier City Council for giving me permission to use the official city photo.

The minutes from the Ranier City Council were an invaluable source of information about the city in the old days. Ted Hall's *Ranier Chronicle* was one of my favorite periodicals and a great source of material about old Ranier. Helen Larson Trask's book *Lake Park School* was very informative about the Jackfish Bay neighborhood and my mother's early life there.

Thank you to the staff at the McIntyre Library at the University in Eau Claire, Wisconsin, where I discovered my Great Uncle Arthur, who turned out to be an integral character in the story. The researchers at the library were very helpful in finding information about Arthur. I will never forget traveling to Eau Claire with my brother Robbie Williams and finding Arthur's and Cora's graves next to each other in the Old Norwegian Cemetery. We didn't give up until we found them that day, even though it was ninety in the shade. Thanks to Robbie for the road trip to Eau Claire, and for his encouragement and support.

The trip up Rainy Lake to Rabbit Island to visit Joyce Christenson and her daughter, Diane Couture Parsons, was not only fun, but invaluable in my research about Fred Couture. Thanks to Joyce, Diane, and her husband Lloyd, for a wonderful lunch and visit. Thanks to my brother Chuck Williams for bringing us to the island that day and for his help and advice while I was writing the story. Thanks to my husband Steve for taking pictures of the island for me and for being there with me that day.

Thanks to Ed Oerichbaur for his help, both as the director of the Koochiching County Historical Museum and as former mayor of Ranier, for his advice while I was researching and writing the book. Thanks to Ranier friends Arden Erickson Barnes and Johnny Walls for meeting with me at the museum. It was so much fun to go through the old pictures of Ranier and sometimes put a name to a face that had not been documented. Thanks to the Koochiching County Historical Museum for allowing me to use photos from the museum archives.

Thanks to Kerry Bickart for letting me use her montage photo of Charlie and Blanche at Kettle Falls in the book.

Thanks to Cathy Brokaw and Mary Dahlin at the International Falls Library for their help in researching Ranier's history through the newspaper archives.

Thanks to former Ranier Mayor David Trompeter and his wife Barb for the wonderful visit, for the coffee, and for sharing some very interesting stories about Ranier.

Thanks to Joanne Finstad for visiting with me and for the information regarding her father's marine business in Ranier. My father looked up to Mr. Finstad and learned a lot about outboard motors from him.

Thank you to Catherine Crawford and my cousin, Sherry Stemm, from the National Park Service for providing me with copies of the oral histories of my parents and of Winston Schmidt.

Thank you to my friend Theo Anderson Dobie and to her wonderful uncle Axel Anderson for talking to me about the Jackfish Bay neighborhood and the Lake Park School, where my mother went to school in the twenties. It was wonderful to hear stories about my mother's neighborhood. Axel is a member of the greatest generation, a true gentleman, and I enjoyed meeting him very much.

Thanks to Jim Bruggeman for helping me to coin the slogan for the book and for his advice and encouragement.

Thanks to Lee Holen for her advice and support, and for editing the book.

Thanks to Nick Nauman, my favorite law clerk, for editing the book and for his words of encouragement.

Thanks to our family friend, Frank Pavek, for sharing information about his grandfather, Mayor Frank Keyes, a good friend to Bob Williams.

Thanks to my sister, June, and my brothers Buck, Robbie, Mike, and Chuck for sharing stories about Dad and Mom and for their love and support. Thanks to Uncle Wayne Jespersen for sharing stories about my mother. Thanks to my cousin Karen from Denmark for her advice and support. Thanks to Bill Dougherty, the lead dog, my brother-in-law and friend for life. Thanks to all of my nieces and nephews for their encouragement and support.

Thanks to my daughters Katie and Stefanie. Thank you to Katie for helping me with the research, for creating the outline with me, and her continued help and support while I was writing the book. Thank you to Stefanie for creating the cover, formatting the photos, for the graphic art designs, and for help with all the technical aspects of the book.

Thanks to all my wonderful friends for their love and support while I was researching and writing the book. Thanks

243

to Debbie and Randy Ciminski for helping with marketing the book Thanks to my friends who read the book and gave their feedback.

Thanks to Mary Casanova for reading my book and for sharing her thoughts and her advice.

Thanks to the great people at the International Falls Daily Journal and North Star Publishing, in particular, Michelle Willmarth and Laurel Beager

Thanks to the wonderful people of Ranier. I hope they enjoy reading about Ranier in the old days.

Finally, thanks to my husband Steve for his help, his love, and his patience while I was researching and writing the book.

About the Author

The youngest daughter of Charlie and Blanche Williams, Peggy Ann Vigoren spent twenty-six summers at the Kettle Falls Hotel, which was declared a national historic site in the 1970s. Her grandfather, Bob Williams, bought the hotel in 1918 for $1000 and four barrels of whiskey. It stayed in the Williams family until the mid-nineties. This is her family's story and is the culmination of many years of research by the author. Peggy Vigoren and husband Steve both live and work in Anchorage, Alaska, where Peggy is employed by the Alaska Supreme Court. Peggy and Steve were both born in International Falls, Minnesota, and graduated from Falls High School together. They have two daughters and a new son-in-law who all live in Anchorage. Peggy and Steve look forward to retirement and summers on Rainy Lake in the not too distant future.

Made in the USA
Monee, IL
24 October 2020